T0129027

She's Sleeping with My Husband

A Novel

Marla Charlie

◖iUniverse®

SHE'S SLEEPING WITH MY HUSBAND
A NOVEL

This is a work of fiction. All of the characters, names, incidents, organizations, and dialogue in this novel are either the products of the author's imagination or are used fictitiously.

iUniverse books may be ordered through booksellers or by contacting:

iUniverse
1663 Liberty Drive
Bloomington, IN 47403
www.iuniverse.com
1-800-Authors (1-800-288-4677)

ISBN: 978-1-5320-4812-8 (sc)
ISBN: 978-1-5320-4813-5 (e)

Library of Congress Control Number: 2018905090

Print information available on the last page.

iUniverse rev. date: 07/27/2018

MOST!

One

⚜

The ride in the long, black limo was melancholy as Joliet sat on plush, dark leather staring out the window, anticipating the day's upcoming event. She looked as glorious as a gorgeous bride could look. Her chestnut-brown hair pulled back, topped with a jeweled crown, made her look like a princess. The bright white veil that cascaded down past her shoulders made her beautiful green eyes stand out, like those of a newly born baby, precious and full of life. Her designer wedding gown exposed her beautifully tanned neckline and nicely shaped arms. It flowed out at her waist, covering both sides of the limousine seat.

Joliet was twenty-two years old, polite, and well mannered. She had just completed the aesthetician course at her local community college. Her dream was to own her own hair salon one day soon. It was said by many of the neighborhood mothers that she would make the perfect daughter-in-law—a catch for any man.

Joliet sat there motionless, remembering all the times she and her girlfriends had fantasized about their wedding days. They would giggle endlessly and share their opinion about the perfect honeymoon and whom they imagined sharing that adventure with. She thought about the night that she and Athena, both twelve years old, had sneaked out her second-story bedroom window and sat on the roof of her home, making plans for their future. They would be each other's maid of honor and take care of each other's babies. They would grow old living next door to each other.

As the long, black car pulled up in front of the massive, beautifully constructed building, Joliet looked up the old concrete steps. This was the church in which she had spent most her life—home away from home, where she had attended school as a child.

St. Marcus was the most respected church in Chicago for two reasons: because the bishop preferred to attend Sunday mass here, and for its history and ornate architectural beauty. Most major events started at St. Marcus—baptisms, communions, graduations, confirmations, weddings, and funerals came and went on this holy ground. Joliet knew everyone coming and going from the church, and they all loved and admired her.

Outside St. Marcus, Joliet could see the joyous bridesmaids waiting at the top of the steps, excited for the bride to arrive. They were dressed in lavish, deep brown, cognac-colored silk. Athena, the maid of honor, stood in the middle of the crowd wearing the same gown, except that hers was tighter fitting and a beautiful sunset-bronze color, identifying her deeper connection to the bride.

Bronze was Athena's signature color because it set off her astounding, long, copper-colored hair. The thick strands flowed down her back like a shining river. Every woman in town had tried to get their hair the same color as Athena's, thinking that might make them as beautiful as her. But Athena's hair color was God given, with just a couple of strands highlighted to a pale gold, further accenting her gorgeous face.

Everywhere Athena went, she would steal the attention of anyone standing nearby. Captivating to look at, her strong, classic features were exquisite, but her sexy charm was also tantalizing. She always stood out from the other girls, like a fluffy little kitten next to a goldfish bowl.

They had planned for the bridesmaids to meet at Joliet's home and get dressed in her bedroom, before riding together to the church in the limo. But an early morning change of plans had left the girls to get ready on their own and meet at the church.

The limo driver looked back at the woman in white, but before he could say a word, Joliet smiled and said, "I know, Jim. I see them coming."

Dressed in a sharp tuxedo, Jim was no stranger to Joliet. A nice-looking man in his thirties, he had worked for her family for years. Jim had married his high school sweetheart, and they had three children under the age of seven.

Jim couldn't help but think something was different about Joliet's demeanor today. She was quite calm—not at all giddy, as she had been on previous days. *It must be all the excitement*, he thought to himself.

Jim got out of the car and opened the door for Joliet. Just then, all the fancy bridesmaids came running down the steps past him, enthusiastic and eager to see the beautiful bride. They all greeted Jim as they climbed into the shiny, black limo with Joliet.

Slumping into the backseat, Rebecca asked, "Jolie, why the change in plans?" Rebecca was a tall, thin blond with pale, freckled skin and a huge smile. "The best part of getting married is the bridesmaids getting dressed and going to the church together." Taking out her brownish lipstick from her small purse, she giggled as she touched up her lips. "Well, not the best part. And weren't your parents supposed to ride with us?"

Staring out the window, Joliet said, "They're in the other limo with my brother. I had some last-minute things to do, and I didn't want to make you girls late."

"For Christ's sake, Joliet, I would have done those things for you," said Athena. "This really screwed things up. We wanted to get dressed together." Athena had been Joliet's best friend since childhood.

Joliet said, "There wasn't anything you could have done, Athena."

Athena told Joliet how beautiful she looked, and the other girls joined in with more compliments.

Joliet's cousin Candice said, "Jolie, I can't believe how unbelievable you look, like a dream."

"Yeah," Athena said, "and tonight she's going to be David's wet dream come true. I saw the lingerie she bought." The girls busted out laughing and Athena pulled out a bottle of expensive bubbly. As she poured it into their glasses, she exclaimed, "Let's get this party started!"

"Yeah!" Rebecca yelled.

"Cheers," they all said, lifting their glasses.

No one seemed to notice Joliet's dismal smile. She was reminiscing about her past, sitting there with her lifelong buddies and remembering the old days when they used to run home from school together, holding hands. They'd laugh and play in the snow, have slumber parties, go shopping, and do all that good girl stuff. She loved David so much, but she couldn't help thinking that her whole life was about to change. Looking at Athena, she said, "You've been my best friend all my life. There's been nobody, except my parents, whom I've loved more than you—not until David."

Rebecca leaned in and jokingly asked, "Jolie, you're not going to ask Athena to marry you instead of David, are you?" The other girls laughed and continued making their plans for the evening. No one was paying much attention to Joliet and Athena's conversation. Everyone already knew how close the two girls were.

They had been inseparable since their first Girl Scouts meeting in the fourth grade. Ten-year-old Athena, a new student, had walked into the Scout meeting wearing a very short, green uniform skirt rolled up too high.

Sister Blithe had yelled at her and decided to make an example of Athena by making her stand in the corner. Joliet had felt sorry for Athena, so as she sat in her chair, she rolled her own skirt up at the waist, just as Athena had done. Then she stood up and walked to the front of the classroom to throw a piece of paper in the trash can. Noticing the inappropriate length of Joliet's skirt, Sister Blithe had put her in the corner next to Athena.

The two young girls had stood there, glancing at each other and giggling the entire hour. After the meeting, they had talked about their unusual names, made plans to visit at each other's home, and become best friends. Ever since then, no one had ever come between them. Now twenty-three years old, they were a nice balance—Athena was daring and self-confident, whereas Joliet was polished and refined. Joliet's family's wealth had made it easy for the girls to share adventure, as part of their lavish lifestyle.

Joliet told Athena how important she and David were to her, and that the friendship the girls shared was one of the most important things in her life.

Athena looked down at her polished manicure and smiled. "I'll never forget the night you met him," she said. "You called me up, telling me you thought he was *so* hot, and you wanted him *so* bad. I thought the little virgin girl was finally going to break down and get some."

"Fuck you, Athena," Joliet whispered, looking away. "Not everyone's a tramp like you."

"Well!" Athena said with a chuckle. "What the hell's the matter with you? Just because I love good-looking men and they love me back? And what a filthy mouth, coming from little miss angel girl." She didn't take any offense at what Joliet said. Kicking off her beaded shoe to check out her perfect pedicure, she just sat there looking gorgeous in her rust-colored gown. The other girls' brown gowns paled in contrast. Hers curved perfectly to her voluptuous body, and her long, silky, reddish hair and orange-red lips made Athena one of the sexiest women most people had ever seen.

Joliet had always admired that about her best friend—that she could be so beautiful and sexy, never demanding attention but always attracting it. Joliet was almost as beautiful as Athena, but since finding David, the love of her life, she had cared about nothing except him.

Joliet had met David by chance, after a long day of shopping and lunch with the girls. Exhausted, she had returned to the mall parking lot, carrying too many bags, and realized that she had locked her keys in her car. Tired and frustrated, she had called the local AAA service—and along came David to her rescue. The two had laughed, flirted, and ended up in a nearby restaurant drinking champagne and falling in love.

As the glamorous bridesmaids sat in the parked limo in front of the church, primping and reminiscing, Joliet couldn't help but wonder if she was about to do the right thing. She had loved David for so long. Family, friends, her beloved Athena, and beautiful David were all Joliet cared about. She had spent the past eighteen months doing nothing but planning for this wedding.

Joliet was awakened from her thoughts when Athena grabbed the glass of Cristal from her. "If you aren't going to drink this," Athena said, "I will. What's the matter with you anyway? I don't see you smiling the way I would be if I knew I was gonna get laid tonight." Athena finished the champagne, then gave Joliet a quick glance with her sultry dark eyes as she climbed out of the limo. The chauffer stood there, lending his hand to help the girls out.

"There's Lauren and Meg," Rebecca said, pointing up the stairs at the other bridesmaids, who were talking with some of the groomsmen and guests.

Athena walked up the steps and flirtatiously greeted friends she recognized. She gravitated to one of the groomsmen and hurried into the church.

Joliet spotted her father waiting for her at the top of the stairs. Joe was a stout gentleman of medium height with thinning gray hair. Extremely charming, he had made his fortune early in life when he helped a friend by buying his failing boxing gym, which Joe then turned into a successful arena for boxers to display their talents. Joe was a smart businessman who always put his family first. He had met Marie, Joliet's mother, one afternoon when she applied for an accounting job. Marie had played hard to get for several months, then finally given in to Joe's persistent invitation. Engaged three months later, they married and had two children, Joliet and Ray, Joliet's younger brother.

The chauffer helped Joliet out of the car and gave her a hug. Then he said, in his strong Chicago accent, "I'll see you in there, princess. Save me a dance."

"Thank you, Jim, for everything," Joliet said. "You and Debbie are always so kind. You're like family to me."

"She's in there with the kids, Jolie, waiting for you," Jim said, smiling. "You know how girls are. They can't wait to see the dress and all that stuff." Then he lifted her chin and asked, "Are you all right, Jolie? You seem a little different today."

Joliet looked at Jim, gave him a strong hug, and hurried up the stairs to her father, her long, pristine train following behind her, flowing over the steps like a cloud. When she reached the top of the stairs, she grabbed her father's hand and kept walking. "I don't want to talk to anyone right now," she told him. "I don't want them to see me."

Joe stopped her as they were walking down the familiar hallway. "We love you, Jolie, and we're so proud of you."

Joliet replied, "I know, Dad. Don't make me cry. I don't want to ruin my makeup. I want to look perfect up there. I want David to remember, for the rest of his life, how beautiful I looked."

Her father just looked at her. No one could have looked more beautiful to Joe than his daughter.

She spotted the ladies' room across the way and said, "I'm gonna slip inside there with the other girls. I'll be fine, Dad, really. See you in a few minutes." She gave her sweet Jolie look and smiled with self-confidence, the way she always did when she knew she was about to accomplish something of importance. "Don't worry so much, Dad," she said affectionately. "Everything will be all right." She walked toward the ladies' room, pushed the door open slightly, and then looked back at Joe and gave him a little smile.

The church was filled with guests on both sides—aunts, uncles, and cousins who had flown in from various places. More than two hundred people waited with anticipation for the family wedding of the decade to begin. Children were dressed up with curled hair, trying to behave themselves. Boyfriends and girlfriends huddled together romantically, excited to see the exquisite bride finally marry her prince charming. Joliet and David were everybody's favorite couple, and everyone was eager to see them finally become husband and wife.

The lovely, delicate sounds of a harp filled the air as guests were being seated. The elegant scent of gardenias lingered in the air, from the flowers that draped the aisles from pew to pew. White gardenias were Joliet's favorite flower and the first flower David had ever given her.

The reception was to be held at the Hotel Monaco, the most beautiful hotel in Chicago. The room was capacious and decorated like an enchanted vision. Tables were topped with pale gold tablecloths and extravagant arrangements of unusual orchids flown in from Belgium for the special event. The floral arrangements stood tall enough on the tables so that guests could easily engage in conversation, and gardenias, of course, were everywhere. Joe and Marie had spared no expense for their one, cherished daughter.

Thousands of tiny lights hung from the ceiling and hundreds of candles swarmed the room, bringing warmth to the ornate setting. An elaborate chandelier attracted attention to an adjoining room, which contained every decadent dessert anyone could desire. The massive wedding cake, at the bride's request, was adorned with the smiling faces of Joliet and David, instead of the traditional bride and groom ornament.

Next to the spectacular cake was an opulent champagne fountain that was sure to satisfy even the most finicky palate. On the other side of the cake was a chocolate fountain surrounded by fruits and cookies—a luscious fondue dessert that Joliet had ordered especially for Athena. The Grand Marnier and cognac bar was a special treat for Joe's boxing buddies, who had all enjoyed that together in previous years. Everything was strategically planned for the reception, and everyone would enjoy the spectacular evening.

Meanwhile, back at the church, the music changed from a single harp to several violins, signaling that the wedding was about to begin. The room got quiet, the lights dimmed, and a side door behind the altar opened. Four groomsmen, dressed in black tuxedos and white shirts, walked out and stood before the guests. Their dark-brown satin ties, made from the same fabric as the bridesmaids' dresses, matched their satin handkerchiefs and boutonnières. Every detail was perfect. Two of the groomsmen were David's close friends with whom he had worked at AAA, and the other two were Mark, David's cousin, and Ray, Joliet's younger brother.

Whispers arose when the best man, Brandon, and David Donnelly, the husband-to-be, walked out. David stood there tall, strong, and handsome with his chiseled, tanned face, dark-brown eyes, and streaked blond, choppy hair. He had a flair for fashion and was the king of his domain in his dark-brown velvet designer tux. David had a lustful smile, and he was enjoying the reaction from several of the young girls sitting in the front pews.

A few moments later, Father Maloney walked out. He had given mass at many events for the Alonzo family—graduations, communions, and even the baptism of baby Joliet.

Then heads turned toward the back of the church to see two little girls dressed in white fluffy angelic dresses and chiffon extending from their tiny heads to the floor. Everyone seemed to be in awe, and one guest could be heard saying, "How precious." The girls held small white wicker baskets filled with gold-sprayed rose petals, which they sprinkled all the way down the aisle as they smiled and giggled.

Then the back doors opened to admit the four bridesmaids. Lauren walked down the aisle first, nervous and excited, as the guests whispered how beautiful her dress was. The bridesmaids' bouquets were made of white gladiolas, David's grandmother's favorite flower. Joliet's cousin

Candice went next, and then Rebecca, whose big, beautiful smile lighted the room. Walking last was Shandra, Ray's girlfriend, a petite girl with black cropped hair—a perfect contrast to the other three girls.

Following a pause, Athena, the maid of honor, came into view looking like a Barbie doll. Her silky bronze dress shined like a new copper penny, and her full red lips seemed irresistible. Everyone stared intently at Athena, and the women admired her as much as the men did. As she followed the other bridesmaids, wearing the same dress but a different color, it was obvious to everyone that she was in a class of her own. Athena walked down the aisle with a certain confident seductiveness that made every woman want to hang on to their date. She was calm, poised, and in control of the room. When she arrived at the altar, she gave a sultry little gesture to the groomsmen and then turned to the guests. The groomsmen looked at each other, smiled, and then turned to wait for the bride.

As the sound of the wedding march echoed through the church organ pipes, the back doors opened once again and the guests stood up. Joliet and her father were standing there, waiting to begin their walk. The wedding planner hid behind them, fluffing out the back of Joliet's exquisite gown. Joe looked at his daughter with reddened eyes, took her hands in his, and asked in a quiet, loving voice, "Are you sure this is what you want to do, honey?"

Joliet warmed her father's hand with hers and motioned for them to begin walking.

The music coming from the organ commanded the attention of everyone in the room. As father and daughter began to walk down the aisle, Jolie's entire body began shaking and her heart pounded in her chest. Walking past the first guests, Jolie kept her eyes focused on the groom, who seemed so far away at that moment. Joe could feel his daughter's hand trembling and clenching his arm, and he wanted to comfort her in some way. If he could only stop and hold her, give her some sort of assurance— but he knew he couldn't. In a few moments, Joliet would set her own destiny. His little girl was about to grow up.

Joliet could hear some of the guests responding to how beautiful she looked. She glanced over and saw Margaret, Athena's mother, standing alone. Margaret was smiling warmly at Joliet, who had been like a daughter to her. She was a tiny woman, in her fifties, with a strong Cuban accent. Athena had inherited her height from her father, who had run off with another woman when Athena was just seven years old, leaving mother and daughter devastated. Athena adored her father and had never gotten over the fact that he gave up his family for his younger, beautiful secretary. Joliet and Athena had met a few short years later, and Joliet had soon become part of the family.

As Joliet and her dad walked farther down the aisle, they passed family and friends dressed impeccably. Guest were commenting to each other about how lovely the father and daughter looked as they walked toward the altar. Joliet was trying desperately to keep her composure as Joe held tightly to his daughter's arm.

As she passed the next pew, Joliet locked eyes with David, the man she was about to marry, the love of her life. He was smiling, amazed at her beauty, as he thought how lucky he was to marry such a gorgeous and wonderful woman.

David remembered the day they had gone running through the sprinklers. He had stopped in the middle of the lawn, water spraying all over them. Soaked to the skin, he had pulled Joliet close to his chest and told her that he didn't want to spend another day of his life without her. Joliet, the girl of his dreams—the woman who would be his wife, give him children, and make his life complete. He felt like the luckiest man in the world.

As Joliet approached the end of the aisle, she saw her mother dressed exquisitely in a beige silk sleeveless gown and diamond necklace. Marie's dark hair was pulled up, and she wore matching diamond earrings. Her eyes were swollen from crying, and she held a handkerchief in her hands. The sight of her mother almost put Joliet into hysterics, but she was determined to keep her composure for this very moment.

When Joliet finally reached her mother, she pulled Marie toward her and gave her a hug. "I love you, Mom," she whispered.

Marie looked into her daughter's eyes, and then held Joliet tightly and said, "I love you so much, Joliet. So, so much."

As more tears welled up in her Marie's eyes, Joliet handed her bouquet to her mother. At rehearsal on the previous night, Joliet had handed the bouquet to Athena, who noticed the change immediately.

Joe pulled Joliet's veil up over her head and kissed her cheek, but then he didn't replace the veil over her face as they had rehearsed.

Joliet climbed the stairs to David and greeted Father Maloney. She then turned to the guests and began to speak in a low, shaky voice. "My friends and family, thank you for being here for us today."

David looked at her in confusion. What was she doing? This was not what they had rehearsed.

"I thank my wonderful parents for this extraordinary wedding," Joliet continued, sniffling a bit. But then she continued in a stronger, more determined voice, "But David and I will not be getting married—not today, and not ever."

Stunned, David exclaimed, "What? What are you saying, Joliet?" He didn't understand what was going on, and people began to whisper.

Joliet grabbed David's hand, then leaned over and took Athena's hand and pulled her toward David as Athena's eyes widened. For the last fifteen hours, pressure had been building up inside Joliet. Like a volcano about to erupt, she couldn't maintain her composure any longer. The enormity and horror of what had happened hours earlier would now be revealed.

"My fiancé, David, and my best friend, Athena, slept together last night after the rehearsal dinner, and I will *never* forgive either one of them!" Obviously upset, Joliet was getting louder. She looked straight at Athena as tears streamed down both their faces, and screamed, "You! I will never, ever forgive *you*, Athena, my best friend."

Then Joliet turned back toward her guests and started down the stairs. Her voice dropping to a whimper, she said, "Please, everybody, go to the reception dinner anyway. My father paid so much money, and there was so much planning." The word *planning* lingered in the air as she ran out of the room in tears.

Mystified, the crowd was shooting daggers at Athena and David as they stood there in disbelief. The entire church was in a state of upheaval. "Oh my God!" Rebecca yelled as she ran down the aisle, trying unsuccessfully to catch up with Joliet. It was an embarrassment beyond comprehension.

Athena paused, and then slowly made her way through the furious, astounded crowd. As she squeezed past one heavyset woman, she caught the eye of her sobbing mother.

"Athena, is it true?" Margaret asked, hoping for some sort of misunderstanding. "It's not true, Athena, is it?" Realizing that her daughter was not defending herself, she cried, "Oh, dear Jesus, no." Then she burst into tears and fell to her seat.

Athena ran out of the church, delirious, not noticing anyone. She passed by the bride and groom's limousine, decorated with "Just Married" and signs of love. Running toward an empty limo, she jumped inside and told the driver, "Get me out of here now. I don't care where we go. Just get me out of here."

She was so punch-drunk that the driver could barely understand what she was saying. He didn't know what had happened—only that whatever it was, it must have been bad. Without a word, he started the car.

Athena sat there in horror, thinking how she had just ruined her best friend's life.

"Do you have any idea where you want to go, miss?" the driver asked.

"No," she said, "just somewhere where no one will find me."

"Oh, okay," he said as he drove away.

Back at the church, family and friends were walking around angry and crying. It looked like a funeral instead of a wedding. Everyone was looking for David, who was nowhere to be found. His mother and father were shattered and trying to console Joliet's parents.

Joe and Marie had been prepared in advance for what took place. The previous night at the rehearsal dinner, their son, Ray, had noticed flirting between David and Athena throughout the evening. He paid closer attention as the flirtation progressed, and he noticed that the two of them were drinking heavily. Ray remembered something similar happening on a previous occasion, which had made him question their credibility at the time. But then he had brushed it off as harmless attraction, until he noticed it again at the rehearsal dinner.

Joliet was busy making last-minute arrangements and didn't notice anything. Even in her darkest hour, she couldn't have imagined that the two people she loved most in the world would betray her that way.

Ray had sneaked up behind David and Athena and caught the end of a conversation in which they mentioned a meeting place behind the old library building. Suspicious, he had followed David after everyone had said their goodbyes. As Ray had approached the old library building, he saw Athena leaning against the wall, smoking a cigarette. David's car had pulled up a few moments later. As David got out of his car and walked toward Athena, Ray had prayed that he wasn't about to see what he knew he was going to see.

As David got closer to Athena, he slowed his pace. She had grabbed his shirt, pulled him close, and begun kissing him passionately. They slid into the deserted old shed, where they spent several hours. A saddened Ray had gone home and told his father, who woke Joliet and gave her the bad news. Heartbroken and hysterical, they had figured out the plan to cancel the wedding and end the relationship.

At the church, the confused guests gathered their belongings. Depressed and lonely, Joliet hid in Father Maloney's office and waited for the hall to clear. She was beginning to realize that her life was going to be a lot different without Athena and David in it. When she had felt sad in the past, she could always turn to Athena for comfort, and after meeting David, there was never any sadness—only sweetness and contentment.

Now, thanks to this catastrophic nightmare, everything had changed. It was like experiencing the deaths of two of the most important people in her world. How could she survive? There was no logic to any of it. This was supposed to be the happiest day of her life, but it had ended up being the saddest. How could they have done this to her? How could David, the man she was going to marry, have done something like that? She and David had loved each other so much, Joliet thought. And she couldn't even begin to fathom the idea that Athena, her best buddy in the world, had crushed her that way. Joliet had loved Athena so much. She just couldn't believe Athena had it in her, to do something so horrible to her best friend the night before her wedding.

Crying harder than she had ever cried in her life, Joliet stayed in the office a few moments more. Then she sneaked outside to the bride and groom's limo and climbed inside. The beautiful luggage packed for their honeymoon, along with the first-class tickets to Italy, were still in the trunk.

Jim, the limo driver, was waiting for her. "I just can't believe it, Jolie," he said, deeply saddened. "Your father told me what to expect when I caught up with him in the church. I can't believe that Athena—or David, for that matter—could do that to anyone, least of all to you."

Joliet's eyes were swollen from crying as she looked up at him. "I can't either, Jim. Will you take me to the airport? I'm going to take that trip anyway."

"Absolutely," Jim said as he started the car. "The trip will do you good, Jolie. Clear your mind and all."

"Well, I don't know about that," she said as she broke into tears again.

"Do you want me to stop? We can stop somewhere, Jolie," he said in his fatherly voice.

"No, I don't know what I'm going to do." Joliet was sobbing, and her head fell to the seat.

Jim pulled the car to the side of the road, got out, and opened her door. Then he reached in and just held her. "You come to our home, Jolie. Debbie and the kids would love to have you over. You can stay as long as you want, until all this shit clears."

It was the first time she had ever heard a curse word come out of Jim's mouth. "Thank you so much, Jim. Thank you, but no," she said, sniffling. "As a matter of fact, I want you and Debbie to take the tickets to Italy."

"No, Joliet," he said slowly.

"Yes," she said, realizing this was the perfect solution. "I'd be miserable there. I need my family right now. You and Debbie take the trip. It's a beautiful vacation, and I want you and Debbie to enjoy it. Bring the kids to my house. They'll take my mind off things."

Jim and Joliet looked at each other. Then she said, trying to force a little grin, "I always love babysitting them. Besides, when was the last time you two took a trip?" The makeup on her big green eyes was smeared.

Jim chuckled and answered, "Not since my kids were born."

"See, that's it. I won't take no for an answer. It's the only thing that will give me any pleasure right now," Joliet said sadly.

Jim argued with her for several moments before finally giving in to Joliet's request. Later that afternoon, he and his wife took off on a jet to romantic Italy.

Meanwhile, a distraught Joliet went back to her parents' home—along with Jim and Debbie's kids—and tried to make some sense of what had happened. It would take a long time for her to heal from such a betrayal, if that was even possible.

David and Athena disappeared as if they had fallen off the face of the earth.

Two

೫ఌఞ

It was a gorgeous autumn day in Canandaigua, New York. The sky was full of orange and yellow leaves, extended from the branches of the proud trees that lined the whimsical, homey streets. The ground was covered with pumpkin-colored leaves that had fallen from the trees, like a blanket warming the cozy town. Nothing could compare to the picturesque setting of upstate New York in the fall.

Canandaigua Lake was known for its pristine beauty and vast size, which made it almost impossible to see its entirety in one day. Getting as cold as twenty degrees below zero sometimes in the winter made the town look like a Christmas postcard.

When spring would arrive, people couldn't wait to get outside to plant and garden. In summer, the town was a dream come true. The locals were excited to finally enjoy the lake, with all its water sports, fishing, and boating.

Only about thirty thousand people resided there, and in a town so small, everybody knew each other. People rarely moved away from Canandaigua, and if they did, they usually moved back eventually. Nothing compares to seeing familiar faces on a daily basis. Everyone cared about their neighbors and would lend a helping hand when needed. It was a perfect place to raise a family—and a perfect place to grow old with someone you loved.

As Kate took the short walk down the street to the neighborhood diner, she thought about how much she liked the unfamiliar surroundings. She had moved to the quaint town from California a few months earlier. She had heard about Canandaigua from some friends and decided it would be the perfect place to take a long vacation. Her plan was to stay in the small community only about six months, and then she would have to get back to her life in Los Angeles.

Canandaigua was not an expensive place, but she had brought only enough money to last six or seven months. Aside from the fact that her family, friends, and everything she loved was back in Los Angeles, this would be an adventurous way for her to meditate about her life and develop as a person.

Kate Rampton was twenty-nine, with a California sunshine look. She was five foot five, one hundred and fifteen pounds, and described by the guys at the gym as a "rock-hard femme fatale." She had a fabulous little body and a honey-colored face.

Kate had a strong sense of herself and loved to be challenged when she had an opportunity to exceed her goals. She had several previous long-term relationships, but she had broken them off upon realizing those weren't the right men for her. She was at a place in her life where she was gravitating toward the fantasy of domesticity, but she was not willing to negotiate her ideals on love. Canandaigua was the perfect place for her at that point in her life—a campground where she could explore her most intimate thoughts, without the influence of her previous relationships.

Taking in a deep breath of chilled fresh air, Kate thought, *This is just what I needed. Getting away from the non-stop chaos of LA is just what the doctor ordered.*

No one in town really knew Kate. She had a temporary job and had made some friends, but no one she couldn't leave behind when it came time to go back home. This extended vacation was turning out to be a great undertaking, an experience she could someday tell her kids about. This was different from the growing experience of her college days. She was almost thirty, independent, and loved the way she felt about life.

From across the street, Kate could see the diner, a hole-in-the-wall restaurant with great food and happy people. A few old cars were parked outside, but most people walked because they lived nearby. Walking toward the diner, she thought how much she loved the simple life of Canandaigua. As she approached the gravel parking lot of the dowdy but adored restaurant, she pulled her unzipped dark-green jacket closed as the brisk air blew softy against her body. It was going to be a cold night.

Kate opened the old wooden door and went inside. The place was packed with people of all ages. Waitresses hurried around, trying to get what they needed. As she stood by the door, the sun shining on her white-blond hair caught the attention of a man about thirty, sitting with a group of friends. There was a glare, and he could not see her face clearly, but he was obviously admiring the color of her hair and the way the sun shone on it and made her look like an angel. As his friends kept talking and laughing, he seemed to be focused solely on the girl at the door.

"May I help you?" the waitress asked Kate.

"Yes, I ordered some food to go. My name is Kate."

"Oh yeah, I think I saw it back there. I'll be right back," said the waitress with a smile.

Kate remained at the door, pulling her gloves off and looking around until she noticed the man looking at her. She took a brief look, thought he was gorgeous, and then reached in her pocket for her wallet.

A few minutes later, the waitress returned with the bag. "You're not from around here, are you?" she asked in a friendly tone.

"Well, no, actually I'm not. I'm from California. I'm just staying here for a few months, sort of a vacation." Kate smiled at the waitress. "I love it, though. Canandaigua is really beautiful."

The waitress agreed as she gave Kate her change.

Tom, the attractive man at the table, was trying not to stare, but he was curious about who she was.

His married friend, who was drinking a beer, looked up and noticed the girl. Nudging Tom, he muttered under his breath, "Wow, she's fuckin' gorgeous. She's definitely not from around here."

Tom didn't say a word.

Kate glanced over and saw the dark-haired man still staring at her. She gave him another quick smile, took her bag, and left.

Tom looked over at his friend as they both chuckled, tapped their beers together, and continued their evening.

The next day was sunny but cold. People were starting to display Halloween decorations in front of their homes, and the town was buzzing about the upcoming Oktoberfest. It was Friday, so everyone in town would be out that night, in the small local pubs that stood on almost every corner.

Tom Verdi had lived in Canandaigua most of his life. After high school, he had gone to a college in Rochester and gotten his bachelor's degree in accounting. Shortly after that, he had enlisted in the army for five years. Both of his brothers were navy SEALs, but Tom, like his father and grandfather, had wanted to be a soldier. Being in the army built strong character and tremendous mental strength, which was something that could not be achieved elsewhere.

Tom was tall, well built, and good-looking, with dark-brown hair. He had beautiful light skin, which complemented his dark-brown eyes. Even more than his looks, however, women loved his sense of humor and charm. But it was obvious by his lack of commitment that he wasn't interested in a long-term relationship, at least not with any of the women from his past.

Tom had two older brothers. Jeff, the eldest, worked and lived in Rochester with his wife and two boys. Jim, who was one year older than Tom, was separated from his wife and lived in Canandaigua near Tom.

Tom had his own home and lived down the street from his mother and father. He taught physical education at the local high school and coached the varsity basketball team.

Tom was relaxing in his backyard, enjoying his day off work, when the phone rang. It was his friend Ryan on the other end.

"Hey, buddy," Ryan said in his deep Irish voice. "You comin' out tonight?"

"Yeah," Tom said. "Who else is going?"

"Everyone."

"Mike B?"

"Yep," said Ryan. "That guy's fuckin' hilarious."

Tom said, with a laugh, "That's why we're bringin' him."

"Pick you up at nine?"

"Yep," Tom replied. They hung up the phone, and the rest of the afternoon was reserved for a nap.

At 9:05 p.m., a car pulled up in front of Tom's house. Ryan honked the horn and the screen door was pushed open almost immediately. In the car were Ryan and his wife, Jill, Mark, Shelly, and the very funny Mike B.

Tom walked out of his house wearing a long-sleeved black shirt, jeans, and black shoes. He was accustomed to cold weather, and he'd often go without a jacket when others would complain about the freezing temps. Obviously handsome, he was starting to grow a light goatee. He wore his black beret, which would usually end up on some girl's head by the end of the evening. Tom was never disrespectful, but he'd always find it amusing when some young woman would end up lying on her stomach, naked, on his bed. She would put the beret on her head slanted, as if she were the first woman to think of doing that. He had seen it at least a half dozen times—that same hat and that same pose. Still, he was a man and thus totally entertained by it.

When Tom got in the car, everyone greeted him. They shared some meaningless conversation about the day, and then Jill started joking about how hot he looked. "You're such a hottie, Tom," she said with a huge smile. They were all good friends, and she often joked with Tom about his life as a bachelor.

"Your wife wants me, Ryan," Tom said. They all laughed and shared a beer, except Ryan, who had agreed to be the designated driver.

Five minutes later they arrived at Grizzly's, the bar they had enjoyed in their younger years. They walked in and noticed that there weren't many people inside.

Tom commented that it wasn't the happening spot it used to be. "Let's get a beer," he suggested, "and then head out to Moonies."

Mike B. replied, "Sounds like a plan."

They all ordered their drinks, had a few laughs, and then left for Moonies.

When they walked into Moonies, the place was packed. The music was loud and everyone was enjoying themselves.

"Man, everybody in town is here," Mark said.

"Yeah, this is it," said Tom. "You guys get a drink. I'm going to the head." Everyone except Tom went to the bar.

A few minutes later, Tom made his way through the crowd to order his drink. When he reached the bar, he couldn't believe his eyes. There she was, right in front of him—the girl, the enticing blond dream who had mesmerized him the night before at the dive restaurant, the woman who was mesmerizing him now. She was bartending at Moonies. *What could be more perfect?* he thought.

Suddenly Tom was excited. He was already having a good time, but now this night was gonna get red-hot. She was working at the bar, which meant that she wasn't going anywhere, so he had the entire night to find out who she was and why he hadn't seen her before.

Tom had never before felt a jolt like this from a woman so quickly. In the past, it had always been the women who wanted Tom. Now it was Tom who wanted this girl. He was immediately attracted to her, and the feeling was powerful.

Kate had light-blond, shoulder-length hair and flawless skin, which held a beautiful glow from riding her bike that sunny day. She was wearing a thin, short-sleeved Rolling Stones T-shirt and short, white, cut-off jean shorts with matching Converse tennis shoes. Her dark, toned legs were the result of long hikes and endless jogs around the neighborhood. She looked fun and sultry, and she was taking her job seriously.

Kate walked over to Tom, looked at him with her heavenly, deep-blue eyes, and said in a cheerful voice, "Here you go." She put in front of him a chilled glass of dark-brown beer, his favorite.

Puzzled, he looked down at the beer as if it were a gift from the gods. "How did you know I drink dark beer?"

She toyed with him a moment and then confessed. "The guy at the end of the bar ordered it for you."

Tom looked over and saw Ryan and the gang laughing. Ryan raised his glass to Tom and whispered across the bar, "That's her, the girl from the restaurant"—as if Tom didn't know.

Tom looked back at the girl behind the bar. She was answering patrons' questions and getting drinks when suddenly a great song began playing and accelerated the mood in the bar. It was a hard rock-and-roll song, familiar to everybody in the room. Most everyone sang along, including Kate.

As she moved around behind the bar, dancing slow and provocatively while making drinks, Tom watched her intently and thought to himself how he wanted to kiss that girl right then. He leaned on the bar as he finished his beer.

Kate was attracted to him as well, with his black shirt, dark hair, and thin goatee. She loved the hat, and she thought for a split second that he would look sexy wearing it naked. But that fantasy disappeared when someone asked for a gin and tonic.

Kate knew that Tom was watching her, and she was enjoying tantalizing him. Something was there from the start, and they both felt it. He would glance over at her, with his dark-brown, tempting eyes, and she would glance back. It was obvious that they were strongly attracted to each other.

She's different, he thought. *She might be the one*. How could he feel this strongly? He hadn't even met this girl, and yet he was fascinated beyond control. He sat at the bar the entire night studying her every move, watching her as she poured drinks and chitchatted with her customers. Every once in a while, she glanced over at him and smiled as he was hypnotized by her gestures.

The night ended with Tom getting Kate's phone number and a dinner date for the following evening.

When the phone rang the next morning, Tom was dead asleep with his face down on his pillow. "Hello?" he managed to mumble.

It was Ryan on the other end of the line. "Hey, buddy, get up," he said in a chipper voice. "It's a bodacious blond day. You have a date with that gorgeous babe. You gotta get out on the lake, get some color for the big night, and if you're lucky, you'll end up naked." Laughing, he added, "You don't want to be bare-ass white, do you?"

"Yeah, well," Tom said in a groggy voice, sounding half asleep, "when she gets a look at my monstrous dick, she's not gonna give a shit how white my ass is." The two and their buddies always joked amongst themselves about their male extremities. "Besides, it's freezing on the lake. I need some sleep. I was thinking about that chick all night." Then he added, under his breath, "She's so fuckin' hot."

"I bet you were thinking about her," Ryan said, "while you were whackin' it."

"Yeah, fuck you." They both laughed. "Although," Tom mumbled, "that's all the action I've been getting lately."

"That's your fuckin' fault, man. You can have all the pussy in this town every night of the week."

"Whatever. I'm gonna go get some coffee. I'll call you back later."

"Hey, where are you taking her tonight?"

Tom paused. "To bed," he said, and hung up.

After Tom showered that evening, he sat on the edge of the bed with a white towel wrapped around his waist. His strong shoulders were tanned from the cold day on the lake. With his hair still wet from the shower, Tom clipped his nails and anticipated the night ahead. He wanted to look great tonight. He wanted the evening to be perfect.

For the first time in a long while, Tom was really excited to go out on a date. He had had relationships in the past, and he had liked—maybe even loved—a woman or two. But something was telling him that this was different. *She* was different. With her, it had been exciting from the start, not knowing her name or where she came from.

Tom knew everybody's name in Canandaigua, where everybody knew everyone and all their business. He liked not knowing anything about Kate. The mystery was exciting, and he wanted to find out a whole lot more about her.

As Tom pulled up in front of Kate's home, he thought about the times he had parked in front of that house before. His friend Shawn had lived there when they were kids, and now this girl was inside that same house. How different it was, pulling up in front of it now.

Tom was wearing black slacks with nice black shoes, a black pullover sweater with white trim, and his new jacket. As he got out of his truck, he looked and smelled great. He stood at her porch, holding a huge bouquet of pink roses, and took a deep breath before ringing the doorbell.

Kate opened the door and said, "Hi" as she pushed open the screen to let him in.

"Hi," Tom replied. He felt his heart racing.

Kate was composed and immediately impressed. She loved that Tom was tall, strong, and charismatic, and that she could sense his nervousness.

Tom's eyes widened slightly as he looked her up and down, trying not to be obvious. She was wearing a black, sleeveless, high-neck sweater dress. Her light hair was pulled up with a tiny white flower, and her perfume was subtle but alluring.

Kate was so different from the other girls he had dated. As he handed her the roses, he said gently, "These are a thank-you for going out to dinner with me tonight."

She took them, and then looked into his eyes and said, "These are so beautiful, Tom. Thank you for taking me to dinner and for the roses." She walked over to the kitchen and pulled out a vase from underneath the sink, filled it with water, and put the flowers in it.

Tom was pleasantly surprised to see that she was wearing high-heeled, black boots. He loved the way they looked on her. Most girls in the neighborhood wore flat boots, so he appreciated her sense of style.

Looking around, he noticed changes that had taken place since the last time he had been in the house. "Wow, the place really looks different."

Kate asked, "You've been here before?"

"Yeah, my buddy Shawn used to live here. I've been in this place a million times, but it never looked like this." He picked up a framed picture of Kate and her mom, admiring it. "I mean it was nice and all, but it just didn't look like this."

Kate had a knack for decorating. The room was filled with candles and pretty pillows, and a little water fountain sat on the end table next to the couch.

Tom liked the tranquil feel of the space. "I love the serenity in here. It's really beautiful." Then he turned to her and said, looking into her eyes, "You're beautiful. You really look gorgeous in that dress and the boots. No one ever dresses like that in Canandaigua."

Kate smiled and said, "Thank you. So do you. I love your jacket—it's sexy."

Tom was caught off guard when she used the word *sexy*, but he dug it. Sex had definitely been on his mind since the moment he first saw her.

They talked for a while, and then he helped her with her coat. They walked out to his car and he opened her door for her.

Over the next few hours, they peeled back years of information about each another and discovered that at the core, they were very much alike. Feeding each other bites of food, they gazed into each other's eyes, sipped wine, and ignored the fact that one day, Kate would go home. They sat there, not realizing that they were falling in love. It would turn out to be a memorable evening—the start of the rest of their lives.

The night ended with a passionate kiss at the front door, and a dinner date at Kate's place for the following evening.

The next day, Kate was up bright and early. She felt happy as she reminisced about the previous night and thought to herself, over and over again, how intriguing Tom was. She really loved his dark hair. As Kate slipped into an erotic fantasy about how Tom would be in bed, suddenly it occurred to her that she might sleep with him that night. "No way! I just met this guy," she said out loud as she giggled. "He's coming over for dinner—and that's it."

Kate started the day with cleaning her small home and throwing her sheets into the laundry. "Why am I doing this?" she argued with herself. "There's no way I'm sleeping with him." When she finished cleaning, she got in her car and took off for the grocery store to shop for the ingredients for a perfect meal. Later that afternoon she prepared some appetizers and set them aside.

Finally she lit some candles around her tub, filled it with water, and got in. She lay there relaxing, thinking about her family and friends back home. Her whole life was in California—everything she owned and loved. *This guy is great*, she thought, *but there's no way anything can happen with him. He lives here and I live there. I'm on a vacation. Yeah, this is just a fun little date*, she reiterated to herself as she dunked her head under the water.

That night, Tom parked his truck in front of Kate's house. As he got out and started up her path, he noticed the front porch lights on and the colorful baskets of geraniums hanging by the door. It looked like such a cozy little home, and he loved the feeling it gave him.

Tom was wearing faded jeans, tennis shoes, and a white long-sleeved Yankees T-shirt. He also had on his navy blue NY baseball cap backward, with his dark hair protruding through the top. The cold air brushed against his clean-shaven face, and he could hardly wait to get inside to see Kate. He was twenty minutes early, but Kate didn't mind. They were excited to see each other, and she had most of the food already prepared.

Kate was surprised to see that Tom had shaved off his goatee. "I like it. You look different," she said, "but you look great either way." He smiled and gave her a kiss on the lips, which led to a harder, more passionate kiss. Wanting to maintain control, Kate pulled away and went over to check the pots simmering on the stove. She knew she was very attracted to Tom, but she didn't want it to go any further.

Barefoot, Kate was wearing her favorite old blue jeans with little tears in them and a white angora, long-sleeved sweater. Her shoulder-length hair was down, and she looked radiant. The living room was lit by candles and a glowing fireplace, which made for a warm house and cozy atmosphere. Dean Martin's music was playing on the CD player, and the setting was romantic.

"Is this Dean Martin?" Tom asked.

"Yes," she answered. "Do you like Dean Martin?"

Tom answered politely, "My mom listens to it. It reminds me of family times when my grandfather was alive. He and I were close. He bought me this Yankees T-shirt the last time we went to a game together. They won, so now it's my good luck T-shirt. Yeah, I love Dean Martin." He smiled fondly, eyes slightly closed, then looked at Kate and said, "It smells great in here."

The table was set with a yellow and pink tablecloth that complemented the flowers Tom had given her the night before. The green dishes were laid out, waiting for the delicious meal that soon would be bestowed them. Kate put the bottle of wine that Tom had brought on the table.

"Dinner will be ready in a little while," she said, offering Tom the plate of assorted appetizers that she had prepared earlier. "I made these especially for you, so I hope you like them."

"Oh yeah," he said when he smelled the aroma of the stuffed little delights. Then he put one into his mouth, and it was obvious that he enjoyed it immensely. "Oh my God," he said, "that's the best thing I've ever eaten! What is it?"

"They're crab balls," Kate said proudly. "My granny taught me how to make them."

Tom stuck another crab ball in his mouth and then tried something else. "I love the way you cook, and I can't wait for dinner," he said with a giggle, still chewing. His enjoyment of the food she cooked was gratifying to Kate.

Throughout dinner, there was a strong sexual tension. They talked about different things—California, Canandaigua, her parents, his parents—but they both felt a constant nagging desire, an excitement to cut to the chase and rip off each other's clothes. Neither one cared about all the other stuff. They *did* want to know all about each other, but later. Right then, all they wanted to do was fuck the hell out of each other, but they knew that waiting as long as they could stand it would make the sex even better.

So they tolerated the conversation, and after dinner they took their wine into the living room by the fireplace. They talked for a while about his coaching job, her place back home, and something else—and then Tom asked if Kate wanted a massage.

Kate was almost thirty, so this wasn't the first time she had been offered a massage. In the dating world, a massage meant that Tom would soon be touching her breasts and they would be getting to know each other a whole lot better. She knew that if she didn't say no, she would hate herself in the morning. But the wine and her desire for him took over her body. "Okay," she said, as if innocent to what it meant.

Tom sat on the couch and moved her over to sit on the floor between his legs. She was sitting in front of the fire, holding her glass of wine. He put his glass down so he could use both of his strong hands to massage her shoulders. He was touching her, and she liked it. Looking at her soft blond hair, Tom fantasized about what he wanted to do next. The feeling in his chest and throughout his body was getting powerful.

"Oh, that feels great," she said nervously as she asked a few random questions about his job.

He answered briefly. Then he leaned in closer from behind and held his face lightly against hers, as his left hand began feeling her body. She could smell his clean skin, and she became aware that he was breathing harder. He started kissing her shoulder with his open mouth, and then she felt his tongue emerge and press against her neck. He slipped his hand down inside her sweater beneath her bra, feeling her erect nipples for the first time. Kate began breathing harder and louder, and their tongues were in and out of each other's mouths, pulsating and driving with strong force.

Tom and Kate were becoming increasingly turned on, and their feelings were getting out of control. She asked him a few more questions, which he ignored. As they became more excited, it was obvious that neither one cared about any more needless conversation. At that moment, it wasn't about him or her. It wasn't about New York or California. It was about sex—and they both wanted it and craved it, insanely, from each other.

Tom pulled Kate around toward him, their tongues pushing together passionately, until it felt as if their mouths were becoming one. The abundance of saliva in their mouths and around their lips was such a turn-on. They were so emerged in the moment that he picked her up and threw her on the couch. She pulled off her sweater, and he pulled off his shirt.

He unhooked her bra from the front, exposing her soft breasts. As he grabbed each nipple softly with his lips, it sent her into an orbit with orgasm. Then he rose up and looked at her face, unable to say a word. The horny expression in his eyes aroused her even more. He shoved his tongue down her throat, and she could feel the strength of his hard cock through his pants.

They were about to give each other exactly what they both wanted—a night like neither of them had ever experienced, a night that only they could give each other, a night that would change their lives forever.

Three

The next morning the sun was barely rising when Kate awoke. She was looking into the eyes of Tom, who had been gazing at her for a while.

Tom was thinking about how beautiful Kate's skin was and how pretty she looked when she slept. He was recollecting every moment of the great sex they had shared the previous night. He had never experienced anything like it with another woman. Who was this girl who had come into his life and so quickly rocked his world? He remembered that she said she would be going back to California, and for a moment he felt nervous about the fact that she might not stay in New York.

Tom was falling hard for Kate. He wasn't sure if it was love, but he knew that she was deep under his skin. After experiencing the intensity of their bodies immersed in such passion, he couldn't imagine an encounter like that happening with anyone else. The night they had just shared had been magical—not just because of the spectacular sex, but also because of the deep connection that was obviously between them. He knew instinctively, especially after sleeping with Kate, that he was feeling something he had never before experienced.

They smiled gently at each other, not knowing exactly what to say. Tom put his hand up to Kate's forehead to move a strand of blond hair from her eyes. "Hi," he said softly. She smiled again. He pulled her gently toward him and they began kissing. The white sheet fell away to expose her breast. Neither of them had any clothes on, and their bodies brushed up against each other. Kate could feel Tom's hard penis on her hip, and it turned her on. Once again, the powerful desire they had for each other took over their bodies, and the morning ended up being just as intimate as the previous night had been.

Later, after Tom left, Kate sat at the kitchen table sipping her coffee. She had a tiny, black, terry-cloth robe on, and she felt extremely happy. It was not just the passionate sex she had shared with Tom; she couldn't remember a time when she had felt so content. She sat there thinking about the time she had spent with Tom and how satisfying it had been. They were so comfortable with each other.

Kate didn't hate herself like she had thought she would. Instead, she felt great about who she was and how Tom made her feel—passionate and alive. *Wow*, she thought, *I've never had sex like that before.* She remembered how his face had looked as he gazed at her breasts. He had been so turned on, and that had turned her on. It was just crazy wild sex. She giggled as she combed her fingers through her blond hair.

Kate liked what she saw when she caught her reflection from the mirror across the room. She chuckled and told herself, as she sipped her coffee, "I'm such a tramp, and I'm finally having some *real* fun here." Tapping her nails on the tablecloth, she thought, *At least I'll have some real great sex before I go home.*

After a moment she noticed the flowers in front of her, and her thoughts deepened. She touched one of them and remembered how Tom had been such a gentleman, opening the door for her and bringing her flowers. He was so polite, and she admired the way he talked about his grandpa.

The feeling turned melancholy when she thought of not seeing him anymore, when it would come time for her to go home. And that time would most surely come. Tom loved the small-town life of Canandaigua. His life was here—his parents, his coaching job, his friends, and everything he loved. *I'm only visiting here,* thought Kate, *and this is happening way too fast.*

She sipped her coffee as she read part of the newspaper and then thought of her job at the bar. *Maybe Tom will stop by,* she thought. Then she remembered she was working the rest of the week. "Damn it," she said aloud as she went to get her schedule and make plans for the rest of the day.

That evening, as Kate was getting ready for work, she chose her outfit carefully. She always wanted to dress nicely for work, but today was different. It was the first time that Tom would see her after that perfect night. She was certain that he would stop by the bar that evening, and she wanted to feel confident about the way she looked.

She knew that nothing would happen that night since she was working late, but it would be a lot of fun to flirt with Tom from behind the bar.

Kate felt great and in control of her life and emotions. She knew that Tom was falling for her, and she liked him a lot too, but she was in the driver's seat. She dug him and wanted to be with him, but she had a plan, and she would have to stick to it. Canandaigua was nice to visit, but there was no way she wanted to live there.

Moonies was out of control that night. It was a popular place because they had the best bar food in town. The music was rocking, and Kate was serving more drinks than she could handle. Later in the evening, everybody was having a great time—singing, dancing, or telling jokes—except Kate, who was in a more serious mood. She was distracted by thoughts of Tom and the evening they had shared. It was almost ten thirty, and Kate was beginning to wonder if Tom would show up at the bar at all. He had never said he planned to be there—Kate had just assumed. Canandaigua was such a small town that there wasn't much to do but hit the local hangouts. She began to wonder if she had been wrong about him.

Her thoughts were interrupted when a guy at the bar said she had just made him the wrong drink. "Oh, I'm sorry," she said, and she smiled and made him a new drink. Then she glanced at the guy to his left … and froze. She wasn't imagining. The beautiful, smiling eyes of Tom were looking right back at her, along with a huge bouquet of red roses. Kate couldn't have been happier to see him.

Tom was leaning on the bar in a way that made him look sexy and self-confident. He had on a heavy jacket, gloves, and a black knitted beanie. He needed a shave and, once again, he looked incredibly desirable. Kate didn't realize until that moment that he was really starting to get a hold on her. His dark eyes were a little more intimidating now as he quietly asked, "Can I have dinner at your place again?" His strong, manly voice had a cunning, sexual undertone.

The two laughed gently, and their eye contact became intense. They were hot for each, and they both wanted another night like the night before.

"What time do you get off?" Tom asked, with obvious intent.

"One o'clock," she said, still staring into his eyes.

"Great." His eyes moved from her eyes, to her thighs, and up and down her body, as if searching for some imperfection that he couldn't find.

They talked and laughed, and Kate was clearly in a better mood than earlier in the evening. Tom waited until she got off work, and then he helped her close the bar. He knew the owner, and everyone trusted Tom. As Kate pulled her gloves on, he helped her with her coat and held the door open for her.

As she walked outside, Kate's eyes widened in surprise. "Oh my gosh, look!"

"What?" he asked, having no idea what she was referring to.

"Look, it's snowing!" Kate answered.

It had started to snow before Tom had arrived at Moonies, but it wasn't new to him like it was to her. In the couple of hours that he was in the bar, the falling flakes had covered most everything in town. Every building and every car was covered with a soft blanket of pristine beauty.

Kate ran outside, romping in the snow. She stood there with a huge grin on her face, holding her white mitten-covered hands out, trying to catch every little snowflake.

Tom smiled at her excitement, but he couldn't share in her joy. He had lived there all his life and seen the snow fall a million times. Still, he loved watching Kate's childlike behavior. When she made a tiny snowball and threw it at him, he smiled and pulled her to the ground. "Lie down," he said, "and put your arms above your head." He pulled her hands above her head, demonstrating what to do. "Now pull them up and down, by your sides."

"Oh yeah," she said, "I've seen this in the movies—snow angels."

They lay on the ground a few moments, smiling at each other and making wings, and then stood up and admired their artwork. Tom put his arms around Kate and drew her close. They hugged tightly, and then he kissed her forehead gently.

"I have an idea," he said as he reached into his pocket and pulled out his keys. "Here," he said, handing his keys to Kate. "Get my truck. I'll be right back." As he started to walk back inside Moonies, he added, "Pick me up at the side door."

He ran back inside the bar and returned shortly, holding a small white takeout bag. Kate had the truck running, creating a huge smoke cloud like a fireplace. She was waiting for Tom with anticipation, unsure of what he was up to. When he got in on the driver's side, she asked, "Where are we going?"

"You'll see," he said with a smile. He drove a short distance and just before arriving at his destination, cut his lights. A few minutes later, he parked his truck in a dark spot and asked Kate to close her eyes. He put an old Dean Martin tape, which he had picked up earlier from his mother's house, into his tape deck. Kate smiled when she heard the lovely music. Tom turned the truck lights on and told Kate to open her eyes. She couldn't believe the incredible sight. With the truck lights on, they could see the snowflakes falling gently over Canandaigua Lake, which was beginning to freeze. Tom had parked in a remote area by the lake, snuggled in between Christmas fern trees.

Kate was almost without words. Finally she whispered, "That's the most beautiful thing I've ever seen." She couldn't get over how amazing it was.

Tom reached behind the seat for his red plaid wool blanket and covered them both with it. Then he opened the little white bag and pulled out two large, white Styrofoam cups filled with hot chocolate.

"Wow," Kate said adoringly, "you thought of everything."

He looked at her with a smile and put his arm around her as they both held their hot chocolates. They sat there as cozy as two lovers could be, looking at the gorgeous vision in front of them. Tom had been in the snow a million times, making snow angels and catching snowflakes in his mittens. He had even seen this beautiful view of the lake before, but not once had it been anything like this. It was as if he, too, were seeing it for the first time.

The rest of the evening was spent looking at the lake as the snowflakes fell gently onto it, and gazing into each other's eyes. Neither Tom nor Kate could decide which view was more beautiful. They stayed there in the same spot until the golden sun rose above the snow-covered lake.

Once again, Tom and Kate got exactly what they both wanted—another spectacular, intimate evening. Much like the previous night, it was an evening unlike any that either Tom or Kate had ever experienced with anyone else. Only this time, there was no sex—just cuddling, smiling, great music, and sipping hot chocolate.

Four

꡷ꕥ꡷

Two months had passed, and Tom and Kate had spent nearly every day together, at either his place or hers. They were together for Thanksgiving, which was the first time Kate met Tom's parents. She got along great with them, and they loved her too. They enjoyed the day spent cooking, drinking, laughing, and pulling a wishbone that left both Tom and Kate wondering what the other had wished for.

After Thanksgiving, Kate saw Tom's mother often, running into her at the bank or supermarket, and even asking her out to lunch. Without realizing it, in a short time she became family.

It was early December, and Kate was walking quickly toward the high school where Tom was coaching off-season basketball. She kept a brisk pace until she entered the gym, and then she sneaked around the bleachers so she wouldn't disturb him. She noticed that the boys looked small next to Tom—so young and immature. They were juniors and seniors in high school, but they seemed a world away from where she and Tom were in their lives. It was nice to watch Tom at work, especially since he didn't realize that Kate was there.

Tom was coaching the young athletes when, in the middle of shooting a basket, a young teenager fell and split his knee wide open. Blood was pouring down his leg and he was in obvious pain. Without hesitation, Tom pulled his favorite Yankees T-shirt over his head and ripped a piece off to make a tourniquet. He wiped the boy's brow with the other part, told him he'd be all right, and then scooped him up and carried him to the sideline, staying calm the entire time.

Kate was about to let Tom know that she was there, but then she hesitated, realizing that he had it completely under control. She was amazed at how smoothly Tom handled the situation. He told one of the other boys to call the injured kid's parents, and then he picked up the kid and left the gym, taking him to the nearest hospital.

As Kate watched Tom leave, she was impressed by the way he had handled the urgent situation—so collected and caring. He had ripped his favorite Yankees T-shirt that his grandfather had given him, without hesitation. He had taken care not to embarrass the boy, who was in obvious pain. Kate was so proud of her new boyfriend, and she felt even safer with him than she had before. If she ever needed his help, he could surely be depended on.

She stood there thinking about Tom and the newfound love they had for each other. She was grateful for meeting Tom, but he had changed the independent life she had been enjoying in Canandaigua. What would happen when it came time for her to go back to California? Would he go with her? Did he realize that she was serious when she told him that she couldn't stay in New York?

Until that moment, everything had been about the adventure. The relationship had been part of all the fun she was having. But now something had happened, and she realized there was no turning back. This was no longer just an exciting experience, but an unexpected fork in the road of her life. She was in love with this man, and she was not going to let him go. How would she approach him about this? How would she bring it up? The smiles, the sex, the falling snowflakes on the lake—Kate was in love, which suddenly made her feel vulnerable.

She left the gym in a doleful mood, wondering how it would ever be possible for her to leave Canandaigua without Tom. What if he didn't follow her—or what if he did? How would his family and friends feel about that? Undoubtedly they would not be happy. After all, she and Tom had found each other in Canandaigua. He loved his mother and father, just as she loved hers. Could she spend her entire life with this man? It was surely beginning to look that way, but also looked impossible to work out. For the rest of the day, Kate pondered her relationship with Tom.

Several days later, Kate was on the phone with her mother, Grace, who wanted her daughter to return home for Christmas. "You have been there long enough, Katie. Dad and I miss you, and Dad's not getting any younger," her mother said, trying to induce some guilt. "You've already missed Thanksgiving, and we really want you to come home, Kate." Then she reminded her daughter that she had intended to stay in New York just six months.

When Kate tried to convince her mother that she would be home soon, Grace reiterated, "You promised that the longest you'd be gone was six months."

Kate replied, "I know, Mom. It's just that—"

"I don't care what it is, Kate," Grace interrupted her. "We want you home."

Kate knew this was not a good situation for anyone. Her parents wanted her home in California and she missed them, but Tom's parents wanted him there in New York. It seemed like an impossible situation that would end with somebody being very disappointed.

Grace had never understood why Kate had gone to New York in the first place, but she had gone along with her daughter's desire to "find herself." But now Grace's patience was running out, and she wanted her daughter back home.

Several times in the previous months, Kate had tried to tell her mother that she might have met someone. But unless that "someone" was coming back to Los Angeles with Kate, Grace didn't want to hear it. Every time, Kate ended the conversation with a promise to her mother that she would return home the following week, a promise that always left Kate feeling sad for the rest of the evening.

The next morning, Kate showed up on Tom's porch with a bag of groceries. "Good morning," she said as he opened the screen door to let her in.

It was obvious that Tom had just woken up. Wearing only his sweatpants and scratching his messy hair, he smiled and said, "What a surprise!"

"I'm making you breakfast," Kate said, walking toward the kitchen.

"Oh man, you're a dream come true." Tom pulled a T-shirt over his head, walked over to Kate, and put his arms around her from behind as she tried to light the stove.

She glanced at him and turned back to the stove to crack an egg. "I talked to my mom this morning."

"Oh yeah? How are things back in Cali?" Tom asked as he flopped onto the couch and flicked on the TV with the remote.

"Well, okay …" Kate hesitated, but then continued. "They want me back home. I'm gonna give my notice to the bar tonight," she said softly, waiting for his reaction.

Tom looked over at her, and the conversation stalled. "What do you mean?" he asked in a calm but concerned voice.

"You know what I mean, Tom. I told you that I couldn't stay here. I don't live here," she said quietly.

Tom couldn't believe what he was hearing.

"I have to go home, Tom," Kate said. "My family misses me, and they need me there. It's almost Christmas."

"What about me? What about *us*? What about *our* Christmas, Kate?" Tom's voice was getting stern, and he was obviously upset.

"You know I can't stay here, Tom. I told you that from the beginning. You knew I was going home in time for Christmas."

"Yes, Kate, but that was before." Tom stood up and walked over to her to stop what she was doing. Putting his hands on her shoulders, he turned her toward him and said, "I love you now, and you love me too. I know you do."

Looking up into his eyes, Kate said, "Yes, but—"

"You can't leave," he interrupted her.

Kate's eyes welled up with tears. "I do love you, Tom, but I have to leave. I don't live here, and this wasn't supposed to happen." She turned away from him and said, "I wasn't supposed to meet you here, three thousand miles away from my family, my life."

"But you did," Tom said, grabbing her by the shoulders and trying to convince her. "We met and we fell in love. Your family has to understand that."

"And what then, Tom? Do I live my life without them?" Kate turned away and said, "No, I can't."

"Can you live your life without me, Kate?" Tom asked, staring into her eyes, waiting, and afraid of her answer.

Kate was silent. Then she turned to grab her purse from the counter and walked toward the door.

"Oh, that's great, Kate," Tom yelled. "Leave, like you planned on doing the whole time!"

At the door, Kate turned to him and said, "Then you come with me. Leave your life here, and come to California to be with me."

He looked at her as if she had just asked him to do the impossible. "I can't leave New York. My family is here, my job, my house ..."

She smugly laughed at him, as if he had confirmed what she just told him. Then she ran to her car, got in, and drove off.

Tom walked back into the kitchen and stood there for a moment, trying to digest what had just taken place—and what it meant. He realized that Kate might actually leave Canandaigua and go back to California, that she had really had a life before she came to New York for a temporary visit. *I don't believe this*, he thought. *She can't just walk out of my life. I love her!*

Since the night he met Kate, his life had finally started to make sense. Maybe there was a future for him—a wife and kids, a family of his own. Until then, he had never thought it possible, but after falling in love with Kate, anything seemed possible. He began to think about his family, his job, and his house. Why should he have to leave New York? He loved the small-town lifestyle of Canandaigua, the solid friendships that took an eternity to build. It was the perfect place to raise a family.

Tom stood there, feeling more and more angry, wondering how Kate could even *think* about leaving their relationship behind. In an outrage, he knocked everything off the counter in one fell swoop. The eggs, the pots and pans—everything fell to the floor as he began to melt down. Then he walked into his bedroom and fell down upon his bed, where he stayed for several hours.

Tom was awakened by the phone ringing. He had fallen asleep after lying on his bed and crying, which he had done only once before, when his grandfather died shortly after giving him that favorite T-shirt.

It was his dad on the phone asking if Tom could help out at the local racetrack. His dad worked at the track and they were short staffed that day.

"Sure, Dad," Tom said slowly. He would rather have stayed home to think things through, but his dad needed his help, and Tom was always glad to lend a hand. So he got dressed and left to meet his dad at the track.

Later that evening he tried to call Kate, but there was no answer at her home. *She must have already left for work,* he thought, and then he wondered if she had given her notice. Tom couldn't imagine Kate leaving Canandaigua in two weeks. It was almost unbearable to imagine a plane taking off for California with her as a passenger. He would somehow try to persuade her to stay—but until then, he wanted to spend every available moment with her until they figured out what to do. He got dressed, stopped at a shop for flowers, and headed out to Moonies.

The small but charming bar was packed with loud conversation, but there was no sign of Kate. Tom assumed she was in the restroom or the storage room in the back, so he waited a moment before ordering his drink. Looking around, he saw some guys he knew sitting at a table and walked over to them.

Making idle conversation, he noticed that two younger girls at the table, who were unfamiliar to him, seemed obviously interested in him. Tom was flattered, but uninterested. He smiled and said to one of the guys, "I'm looking for my wife."

"Your wife?" his friend said with a laugh, sipping his beer. Then he looked at the girls and joked, "If you knew this guy, you'd know how funny that is. He'd be the last guy in this bar to get married."

Now the two girls were even more intrigued. One of them said to the other, "If she doesn't show up, I'll take her place." They giggled and continued with their evening.

Tom casually turned away and walked toward the bar. He ordered a beer and then realized that the new bartender, Rob, was working on his usual day off. "What are you doing here?" Tom asked as he sipped his beer. "Isn't Thursday your night off?"

"Yeah, but that girl Kate quit," Rob said. "So Mike asked if I could cover her shift."

Suddenly Tom was focused on every word the bartender spoke. He put his beer down and asked, "What do you mean, she *quit*? Kate's not coming back?"

"I guess not. I think she caught a flight back to California today."

Horrified, Tom shoved his way out of the packed bar as Rob shouted, "Hey, weren't you two—?" Then he noticed that Tom was already halfway out the door. "Whatever," he mumbled to himself as he wiped down the counter.

Tom couldn't get to his car fast enough. Fumbling for his keys, he was in a panic. He drove fast, breaking the speed limit as he tried desperately to reach Kate's house. He was adamant, all the way to her house, that he *would* move to California. Of course he would! After all, what was the alternative? To live without Kate in his life? That thought was painful. Tom was a man who knew what he wanted—and he wanted Kate.

He hit a red light. "*Shit!*" he yelled as he pounded the steering wheel. He had made up his mind. When he reached Kate's home, he would fall down on his knees, grab her hand, put it to his heart, and ask her to marry him. They would go to California and have a great life together. He wanted a home with twenty kids who all looked exactly like Kate. And they would live there until they were a hundred years old, just like his parents. All the way to her house, he was realizing that he loved Kate much more than he had known. "I'll never love anyone as much as I love Kate. Never. I'll do anything and everything it takes to make this work."

Driving up Kate's street, he could see her car parked beside her house. With a sigh of relief, he pulled quickly into the graveled driveway. Leaving his truck parked half in the street and the door open, he raced up to the front of the house yelling, "Kate! Kate!" He pulled open the screen and pounded on the front door. "Kate!" He went to the side of the house and pounded on a window. "Kate!"

The house was dark, but the moonlight allowed Tom to see inside. There were things missing, little things like candles and the picture of her grandmother. And there was what appeared to be a letter on top of the coffee table, held in place with a little vase of flowers. He ran to the back of the house, remembering a broken hitch on the back window. He pulled on it, yanked it open, and crawled inside.

He flicked the light switch, but Kate had already had the electricity shut off, so he lit a candle that he found discarded in the trash. Walking through the house that Kate had lived in, Tom realized the depth of the love he felt for her. His heart sank as he reflected on the times they had shared in her home. The night she had cooked him that delicious meal. The night he had fallen in love with her.

He walked upstairs and stopped when he entered her bedroom. The first night they spent in there and the nights that had followed had been the best nights in Tom's life. Not because of the sex, but because of the love he and Kate had expressed for each other.

He walked over to the closet and opened the door. Only a few empty hangers hung inside, and he realized Kate had really left. His head fell in sorrow. As fast as she had come into his life, she was gone. Then he noticed something in the corner of the closet. Bending down to pick it up, he realized it was her little white angora mitten. She had been wearing those mittens the night she first saw snow fall outside of Moonies Bar. He remembered how excited she had been, trying to catch every snowflake with her hands, covered with those mittens. Those precious mittens had flapped at her side as she learned to make snow angels with him. She had such a huge smile on her face, showing all her teeth. Her head had been covered in snow. Maybe that was when he fell in love with her.

Tom held the candle closer to the mitten and could see a little stain on the fingertip. He realized it was a drop of hot chocolate that she had gotten on her mitten when they sat in his truck beside the snow-covered lake. They had been sharing childhood stories and gotten to laughing really hard. After taking a sip of his hot chocolate, he had had a little drip on the side of his mouth. She had wiped it gently with her mitten-covered hand, staring deep into his eyes. Then she had snuggled into his arms like a newborn baby—and maybe *that* was when he fell in love with her.

Tom fell to his knees like he had planned to do, but he didn't get to hold her hand next to his heart. He began to sob as he felt the pain of her absence, and he regretted that he hadn't told her sooner. It was now so obvious to him how much she meant to him, and he could no longer ignore it. He realized that it didn't matter to him where he lived or what he did. His home was wherever Kate was. His life and his love were Kate. Where she lived was where he wanted to be.

Tom hadn't known Kate long, but he knew that he was feeling the real thing—and he was ready to make that decision in his life. She was the woman with whom he wanted to spend the rest of his life. Kate was his family now. His future was with her, and if that meant living in Los Angeles, then he would do so with open arms, rather than live his life without her. He would tell his family and friends in the morning, find someone to replace him at work, and put his house up for sale. Tom had made up his mind, and he was moving to California.

Five

Tom spent the entire flight to Los Angeles preparing for his new life ahead. He sat there in his jeans and black jacket, reminiscing about past events with Kate, fantasizing about what their future would look like. He was surprised at how extremely supportive his family and friends had been, and he was quite relieved by their reaction to his news.

His brother Jim had offered to move into Tom's house for a while, to give Tom time to figure things out. Even the athletics director at the high school had told Tom how much he appreciated Tom's dedication to the school, and that he would always have a job there if he should return. Everything was in place, and Tom was ready to embark on his new life in California.

When Tom arrived at LAX airport, it was late afternoon. He was amazed at how warm the weather was in the middle of December. He had just left a snow-covered town in New York, so the sixty-eight degree temperature in LA was a nice change from the ice-cold air in Canandaigua.

He unzipped his jacket, took a look around the terminal, and headed in the direction of his luggage. After retrieving his belongings, Tom caught a cab and left for Ventura. "Thousand Oaks," he told the cabby.

"Thousand Oaks is one of the safest cities in the country," the cabbie said proudly.

Tom smiled as he peered out the window. "Yeah, that's what she told me." Conversation was minimal for the rest of the trip. Tom wanted to focus on his approach to searching for Kate. He had no idea where she lived, only that she often referred to the town as TO.

After Tom briefly described his reason for being in Los Angeles, the cabbie was eager to help him. An older native of California, he took Tom to a centralized landmark hotel in a nearby city, which he thought would be most convenient for his search. Tom thanked the cabbie with a generous tip and checked into the hotel. He decided that he would get situated and then make his first attempt to find Kate by combing through the phone book.

Frustrated upon finding that she was not listed, Tom decided to get some rest and make a fresh start in the morning. He ordered some food, watched a little TV, and then fell asleep, exhausted and eager to find Kate.

The next few days proved to be exceedingly frustrating for Tom. He was no closer to finding Kate than the moment he had arrived in LA. He visited every beauty supply store in town, since he couldn't remember the name of the one she worked at. He went to restaurants and bars, and he showed a picture of her to everyone, but no one had ever heard of Kate Rampton. He was beginning to feel presumptuous about thinking he could find her in such an enormous place. *You can find anybody in Canandaigua,* he thought. *If someone's looking for you, they'll find you.*

He was sitting in a breakfast restaurant, starting to think he'd never find Kate, when a waitress made a suggestion. He mentioned that Kate had a small house in Thousand Oaks, and the waitress told him to go to a real estate office and have someone look up her house by name in the CRISNet registry. Tom was so ecstatic with the waitress's suggestion that he gave her a twenty-dollar tip and kissed her on the cheek.

She yelled out to him while checking out her generous tip, "If you don't find her, come back in." Then she smiled as Tom walked quickly out the door.

Tom drove to the nearest real estate office and gave the receptionist the information she needed to look up Kate's house. Impressed with his strong, masculine voice, the receptionist dialed the extension of the real estate agent, whom she believed would surely be happy to help him.

When the agent walked up to the front desk, she was not prepared for the studly man who stood before her. With a flirtatious smile, she asked, "What is it you need?"

"I need you to look up someone's home address for me," Tom answered. "I'm in town, but I've forgotten my friend's address. I've looked in the phone book and tried everything else that I can think of."

She looked at him, wondering about his true intent. "Well, what exactly is it that you're trying to find out?"

"I'm desperately trying to locate someone," Tom said, "but I don't have their address."

Backing away a bit, the woman said, "Oh, I can't do that. It's against real estate politics, and I could lose my license."

Tom realized that he needed to be more persuasive with this woman in order to get Kate's address. He leaned toward her and tried to use every ounce of his tall, dark, and extremely sexy charm. Looking at her with his dark, piercing eyes, he said, "Come on, gorgeous. You don't look like the kind of girl who's afraid to take a risk. Just help me out here, and I promise I'll return the favor someday."

Just like that, the agent was on the computer looking up Kate's address. She was disappointed that Tom had given her a woman's name, but she was still willing to help him out. Entering bits of information, she asked, "Does this woman have a middle name?"

"Oh shit, I can't remember it," Tom answered.

After a moment she asked, "Could it be Elizabeth?"

"Yes!" he replied with excitement.

"Here's the only one I have in Thousand Oaks," she said as she wrote the address on a small piece of paper. "Katherine Elizabeth Rampton and Christopher Ronald Rampton."

"Christopher?" Tom asked in an annoyed tone. "Who the hell is Christopher?"

"Well, according to this, he's her husband. When was the last time you saw this great friend?" she asked.

Tom's face dropped as both women looked at each other with widened eyes. "What the fuck?" he said, not caring who heard it. "She's been living in New York for the past six months, and she never said anything about being married."

The receptionist at the desk muttered, "They never do." The girls looked at each other and giggled.

Tom didn't think it was funny at all. "Does it say anything else there?"

The agent responded, "No, just that they have owned the house for almost two years, and the real estate information."

Kate's urgency to get back to California started to make sense. Tom was running everything over in his head. Feeling foolish and betrayed, he was reluctant to take the address, but he asked for it anyway. After he got the information, he started to walk out without even saying goodbye. But then he turned back toward the girls and asked, "Could you give me directions to this place?"

Understanding his frustration, they wrote the directions down for him. The agent then reached in her drawer and pulled out her business card. "If you get stuck without a place to stay, give me a call and you could stay at my place—on the couch, of course," she said as she smiled at her friend.

"Yeah, well, whatever." Tom paused and then added, "Thanks" as he walked out the door. He threw the card in a trash can outside when he knew they could no longer see him. "Yeah, I'll call you all right," he said under his breath. "Fuck you," he whispered, really aiming his remark at Kate.

Pissed off, he drove away with the directions in hand. "Where the hell is this place?" Tom said to himself. After a couple of wrong turns, he finally came to a sign that read "Callaway." "Here it is," he said, driving down the street trying to find number 1407. He wanted to see the house Kate lived in, and he knew he was getting closer. "Let's see: 1424, 1418 ..."

Tom saw an old man watering his lawn, reminding him of the old guys back home. So he pulled his car over, rolled down the window, and asked, "Excuse me, do you know a Kate and Christopher Rampton?" As the old man walked over to the car, he reminded Tom of his grandfather. On a better day, Tom would have struck up a conversation with the old guy, but he was in no mood for that now.

The old guy looked at Tom for a moment, and in a shaky voice said, "You're looking for Kate and Christopher?"

Tom answered, "Yeah."

"Right down there," he said as he pointed to the yellow house.

"They both still live there, huh?"

"Yeah, I think so. I think Kate went back East for a while, but she's back now."

Saddened, Tom was eager to get out of there. "Thanks, old-timer," he said with a weak smile.

Tom drove down the street and pulled up in front of the cute yellow house. He took a moment to stare and wondered why she had never mentioned being married. He wondered if there were kids. Maybe Kate and Christopher were separated, trying to work things out. Whatever their problems were, he didn't want to be a part of them. He would have to lick his wounds and go back to Canandaigua.

How could she have done this to him? Did she care for him at all? Suddenly this woman was a stranger—with a husband. She already had a life, and she had seriously misled Tom. Now he knew why she couldn't stay in New York. She had to get back to California because of her *family*? He had never dreamed that her family included a husband and kids.

Thinking about how had he left a great job, his family, and friends, Tom realized he really didn't know this girl at all. *Serves me right*, he thought. "Shit!" As he started to drive off, a car coming from the opposite direction passed him. He noticed in his rearview mirror that the car was pulling into the driveway of the yellow house. Something inside him was excited seeing the car, even if it meant it would be the last time seeing anything that had to do with Kate. He wanted an explanation before going back to New York, so he stopped his car.

A young, blond-haired man in his early twenties got out of the other car. Not as strong-looking as Tom would have imagined.

You've got to be kidding me, Tom thought. *This guy's a douchebag. Look at him.*

The guy noticed Tom's car, but paid no attention to it and went into the house.

"What the hell," Tom said, trying to make some sense of the frustrating situation.

A few moments later, the guy came back outside to his mailbox.

Tom put his car in reverse and backed up to the yellow house. "I've gotta talk to this asshole," he whispered to himself. "Excuse me," he called out the window.

"Yeah?" the guy answered.

"Is there a 1486 Callaway?" asked Tom.

"Gee, I don't know. I guess there could be," the blond guy said in a weak voice.

God, no wonder she came to New York looking for me, thought Tom. "Well, I've been all around here, but I can't find it," he said, stalling for time while he tried to figure out why Kate even liked this guy. "Maybe one of your kids knows, or maybe your wife?"

"Well, I could ask my wife, if I had one."

"Oh, getting divorced?" Tom asked.

"No, I've never been married." Then he mumbled something that Tom couldn't quite hear.

"Wait, what do you mean? You've never been married?" Tom asked. "Isn't Kate your wife?"

"Kate's my older sister," the blond guy answered with a laugh. "I'm Christopher. Who are you?"

Tom quickly parked his car and jumped out. "Oh my God, man! You can't believe what I've been going through, trying to find your sister!"

"Who the hell are you?" Christopher asked.

"Wow," Tom said as he looked up at the sky in obvious relief, genuflecting and thanking God. Then he shook Christopher's hand and said, "I'm Tom. I met Kate in New York." He was talking in a much faster, more excited voice than before.

"Oh, you're the dude she's been talking about to my mom." Christopher now understood the change in Tom's tone of voice.

"She's talked about me?" Tom asked curiously.

"Yeah, talked and cried. I guess she didn't want to leave Calangagna, or wherever the place is you guys live."

Tom laughed and said, "That's Canandaigua."

"Whatever. Kate hasn't been living here since she got back. She's been living with my grandma."

"Where is she now?" Tom asked.

"She's at the store," Christopher answered. "She works at the beauty supply store."

"What's the name of the store?" Tom asked. The million-dollar question—he'd been trying to remember that name for three days.

"Beauty on Request."

"Oh God," Tom sighed, "that's right."

"But hey, if you really want to surprise her, wait until tomorrow to show up. It's her thirtieth birthday."

"Are you serious man?" Tom asked. "I can't wait another day to see her." But then he paused and gave it serious consideration. "Although that would be really cool. Don't say a word to her then, okay?" He smiled, thinking about what was going to take place the following day. It would be perfect. After all, he had already waited this long.

Tom now had a different perspective on this guy. He was gonna be family someday. He wasn't douche—he was a brother-in-law! He hugged Christopher and shook his hand.

"Nice meeting you, Tom," Christopher said. "I can't wait to see my sister's face when she sees you."

Tom replied, "Man, you have no idea." He got in his car, waved out the window, and drove off with a smile on his face.

That night, Tom tried to get to bed early, but he was restless and couldn't sleep. Suddenly, he realized he didn't have his birthday gift. He called the front desk and asked for a wakeup call for eight o'clock.

The following morning, Tom visited several jewelry stores. Finally he found a beautiful cluster ring with a huge round diamond in the middle. The ring was spectacular. Something about it reminded him of the snowflakes in Canandaigua, and immediately he knew it was the one.

Without asking the price, he told the jeweler, "Wrap it up." Tom had never been impulsive or irresponsible in making large purchases, but he realized this was a once-in-a-lifetime event, and he was not going to compromise now.

As Tom was at the counter waiting for his purchase to be wrapped, he looked at the Christmas ornaments hanging from the ceiling. He noticed one in particular and asked the jeweler if he could buy it. The jeweler put it in the bag with the ring.

Tom felt great about his gift. He left the store confident, heading for Beauty on Request, where the woman who would wear that ring worked.

As he pulled in at the shopping center, Tom noticed a corner bakery and got an idea. The pastry shop was filled with decadent desserts, but he went straight over to the cake section. In the window sat a miniature wedding cake—small, but big enough to make an impression. "I'll take that one," Tom said. "Is there anyone who could deliver this over to the beauty supply store?"

Marge, the older robust woman behind the counter, glanced over to where Tom was pointing. "Oh, is this for Kate? Today's her birthday."

"Yes," Tom answered.

"Oh, then you don't want this cake, honey," said Marge. "This is a wedding cake, not a birthday cake."

Tom smiled and said, "Yes, I know."

"Oh my gosh! Of course we can deliver it," she squealed. "I'll deliver it myself." Marge, a major stockholder in gossip, loved Kate and knew about all her drama with her boyfriend. She would make every effort to ensure the cake was decorated perfectly and delivered promptly.

Tom went out to his car and got the engagement ring and the Christmas ornament, which he gave to Marge to be used as special cake decorations. She left a few minutes later, and he waited eagerly as the cake was delivered.

A few stores down, the doorbell rang in the beauty supply store, announcing that a customer had just entered. Kate peered from behind the counter, looking great in a white sleeveless sweater, faded jeans, and black high-heeled boots. There was a little pink flower in her blond hair.

"Happy birthday, Katie," Marge said with a smile. She held out the pink bakery box, unable to wait another minute for its unveiling.

Tom waited outside, just around the corner, and tried to hear what was being said.

Kate was excited at the sight of the pink box. "Thank you, Marge. You're so sweet." She walked from behind the counter and kissed Marge on the cheek. As she took the box, she started to ask Marge an unrelated question, but—

"Open it up, Kate!" Marge insisted.

"Oh, of course," Kate said, giggling with anticipation. She cut the tape on the pink box. When she opened it, she paused as it took her a minute to realize what she was seeing. There sat a small white wedding cake with a snowflake ornament on top. In front of the ornament was a gorgeous diamond engagement ring and pink writing that read, "I found my snowflake. Will you be my wife?"

Speechless, Kate stared at the cake, thinking that the unbelievable had come true. She had been crying for days, wondering if she would ever see the love of her life again. And he was here, asking her to marry him. She wanted nothing in the world more than to do just that.

An overwhelming feeling of happiness ripped through Kate's body as she looked around and shouted, "Oh my God!" Crying uncontrollably, she ran out of the store, searching for Tom. As she turned the corner, she ran straight into the man who loved her.

Handsome with his dark hair and green sweatshirt, Tom gently stopped her and sweetly just said, "Hi." He knew, by Kate's reaction, what their future would be. Engulfed in his arms, she kissed his face over and over again. He felt her tears mix with his own, their love for each other pouring out as she said, "Yes."

It was evident to everyone at the wedding that Tom and Kate were deeply in love. The wedding took place outside, overlooking the ocean. The ceremony was simple but memorable, with the bride and groom, both teary eyed, pledging their vows to each other.

The reception was a lively party attended by their family and closest friends. Even the funny Mike B. flew in from New York. Tom's mom, dad, and brothers sat at the same table as Kate's family, rather than the traditional reception table seating, so that they could get to know each other better.

Kate sat close to her new husband, smiling as they sipped their champagne and toasted each other. She was luminous in her tank-top-style gown, which was form-fitting white silk. She wore her blond, chin-length bangs parted in the middle, framing her gorgeous blue eyes. Her hair was in curls, piled beautifully on top of her head. Behind the curls, Kate wore her grandmother's ornate diamond cluster broach, which was "something borrowed." Tom wore a black tuxedo, his goatee, and a devilish grin for his new bride.

Everyone admired the two large wedding cakes, which were a surprise gift from Marge at the bakery. One was in the shape of New York and the other was the shape of California. An edible bridge connected the two cakes, with a scrolling message that read, "Kate and Tom—to the ends of the earth to find each other."

The happy, bicoastal couple never stopped beaming that evening. They giggled all night over everything—the goodies, gifts, anything that caught their eye. Most of all, they enjoyed meaningful words from the people who loved them. Everyone had something wonderful to say about the bride and groom. Kate's brother, Christopher, told the funny story of the first day he met Tom outside his home, and everyone laughed. Tom laughed the loudest when Christopher talked about the part where Tom had thought Kate was his wife.

Tom wrapped his arms around Kate and yelled with pride, "She's my wife now!" Everyone cheered and chuckled. Kate had a huge smile on her face as Tom kissed her cheek. They felt like the two luckiest people in the world, to have found each other after all the odd circumstances.

The evening ended with more cheers and someone toasting, "To long-lasting love and all it has to offer." Everyone lifted their glasses as Tom and Kate kissed each other on the lips.

In their first year of marriage, Tom and Kate worked really hard to get their life together off to a good start. Tom went back to school at a local community college, working toward a master's degree in accounting. He had already gotten a good jump on it back in New York before he met Kate, but then he had gotten distracted with his coaching job. Now he only needed to complete a few more classes, and he was working night and day to achieve that goal.

Meanwhile Kate pulled out equity from the house she owned with Christopher to purchase the beauty supply store, which had been for sale for quite a while. Paying it off would take them approximately three years. Kate had wanted to buy the store for a while, but it just hadn't been the right time. After meeting Tom, however, everything seemed to be falling into place and all their dreams were coming true.

Tom went to work for a local accounting firm, with the intent of opening his own office in the second year. They had their financial goals in place and were working hard to achieve them.

It was the evening before their first anniversary, and Kate couldn't wait to give Tom his gift. She had been so excited the entire week, counting down the hours until the actual day. She had gotten off early from the store, and Tom had just called to let her know he was on his way home. Kate was busy in the kitchen cooking a glorious dinner, which was a carbon copy of the meal she had cooked on that memorable first night they were together.

Tom and Kate lived in a one-bedroom town house, decorated modestly with pictures of the two of them everywhere. On top of their stove was a picture of them with Hawaiian leis around their necks, taken on their honeymoon.

Kate was mixing the ingredients for the crab balls when she heard Tom's keys wrestling the lock at the front door. She put down her spoon, wiped her hands with a towel, and ran to the door to greet her husband.

After a year of marriage, Tom's sex appeal was getting stronger every day. He was happier and more self-confident than ever. His dark hair was a tad longer, and his style was enhanced by California living. He had joined Kate's gym, where the two of them went on a regular basis. He was more devoted to his wife than ever.

He walked through the door wearing beige dress pants and a button-down, short-sleeve, raw-silk shirt, and he smelled great.

Kate adored her new husband. "Hi, baby. Happy anniversary eve," she said as she threw her arms around him and kissed him passionately.

The room was lit just like on the night of their first intimate evening. The amber glow of candles burning, next to the fireplace and throughout the room, created a romantic ambience. The plaid, red wool blanket from the night in front of the snowflake lake rested on a chair in front of the fireplace, where a fire burned brightly. The home smelled of a delicious meal cooking in the oven.

"Wow, what smells so good?" Tom asked as he dropped his briefcase and put his arms around her.

"That's me," she joked.

"I know that's you, sexy woman," he said as he snuggled into her soft, blond hair and kissed her neck. "What's this you've got on?" he asked as he put his fingers underneath the thin, pale-yellow strap and played with it.

She was wearing a flimsy, see-through nightie, and it was evident by the outline of her breasts that she had nothing on underneath. Her thin, shapely legs stood out from beneath the short little baby doll gown.

Tom was obviously admiring her body as he devoured it with his eyes. "I love you," he said, sucking her neck. "Ooh, you're so hot."

Then the timer on the stove went off and Kate pulled away. She walked over to the oven and turned off the buzzer. Then she went back into Tom's arms.

Tom got distracted by the delicious smell coming from the kitchen. "What's cooking?" he asked as he glanced over at the stove.

"I made us a special meal for our special anniversary."

"Our anniversary's not until tomorrow," he said, pulling both her straps down and wanting to make love to her.

"Well," she said, with a devilish grin, "I wanted to start celebrating early."

"In that case, I've got a present for you," Tom said, wanting to give her his manhood.

"Oh no," Kate said, in a sultry tone, "give it to me tomorrow. I'm gonna give you your gift tomorrow morning." She slid her hand down to his crotch, where she could feel his dick getting harder.

"No, I'm gonna give you your gift tonight," he said, and started kissing her hard on the mouth.

They were enjoying the moment, but then Kate pulled away. "I've gotta get this stuff going, or we won't have crab balls tonight."

"Crab balls? I love those fuckin' things!"

"Tom!" Kate said, frowning at his choice of adjectives.

"Sorry," he said, "it's just that I love those things so fuckin' much." They both smiled.

Tom walked over to the refrigerator and took out the bottle of champagne. He looked at it, but then put it back into the fridge and said, "I'm gonna go put on my sweat pants. I'll be right back."

Kate smiled. "Go ahead, honey. These things will be done in a little while." She stayed in the kitchen preparing the rest of the dinner while Tom went into the bedroom to freshen up and get comfortable.

A few moments passed and then Tom returned, wearing a white T-shirt and dark blue sweatpants. He was caring a medium-sized white box, which seemed slightly heavy, with a red bow on top. With a huge smile on his face, he said, "I've got your present here."

Kate immediately turned around, dropped the spoon, and walked over to Tom and the box. "What is it?" she asked, with an enormous grin on her face.

"Open the box," Tom said. As Kate started to take the box from him, he stopped her. "I'll hold the box," he said, "and you take the lid off."

Kate was so excited. "Okay. This reminds me of when Marge came into my shop on my birthday and I … Oh my God! Oh my God! He's so cute." She reached in and pulled out a solid white, wrinkled little puppy. "He's the cutest little thing I've ever seen," she said.

The puppy was tiny, fat, and soft all at the same time. He looked like a little snowball, with his dark eyes peering through white eyelids and his pink tongue sticking out of his mouth. His face was wrinkled and his white ears hung off the sides of his little head. Obviously scared, he sat without moving as he looked at Kate, who couldn't take her eyes off him.

"It's all right, little fella," she said adoringly, gently rubbing his chin with her finger. He was precious.

"He's an English bulldog," Tom said proudly. "He's very rare."

"Oh my God, I love him, Tom." Kate had tears in her eyes. "He's the best, cutest little thing in the world. I love him, honey. Thank you so much. I love you, Tom." She kissed Tom, then the puppy, then Tom, then the puppy—over and over again. She was lost in the excitement and obviously elated. Tom was pleased.

They sat in front of the candle-lit fireplace with their red-plaid blanket on the floor and their new puppy on the blanket. Then Kate looked up at Tom, and said softly, "I want to give you your present now, Tom."

"I thought you wanted to wait until tomorrow morning," he said in a studly, teasing voice, while rubbing the puppy's belly.

"No, I'm gonna give it to you now. I'll be right back." She left for a moment and went into the bedroom.

When she returned shortly after, she was standing in the hallway with one arm above her head, leaning against the open door. She was relaxed, totally nude with a huge bow wrapped around her waist, looking extremely voluptuous.

Tom was playing with the docile puppy when Kate said, "Tom-my." He looked up and saw his wife standing in their bedroom door, with a pink and blue bow wrapped around her waist. He stared at her for a moment, loving the fact that she was naked, but the excitement of the bow took over his emotions. She smiled, and he got up off his knees.

He asked softly, "Kate, are you pregnant?"

"No, *we're* pregnant," she said.

They looked at each other, loving the moment and each other, ecstatic over the new changes in their lives. Since the day Tom and Kate met, things happened rapidly for the two of them, and they both loved it. They were so in love with each other and had waited so long to finally find each other, that they already knew what they wanted—a life and a family, together.

They hugged and loved each other for the rest of the evening. Then Tom, Kate, the puppy, and the baby-to-be all fell asleep together, a growing and happy family, the Verdis.

Six

It had been more than three years since Natalie had been born. The ribbon of new ownership was being cut in front of Beauty on Request. Tom stood in the crowd by the store like a happy spectator, holding their adorable one-year-old son, Tyler, who was the spitting image of his mother. Dark-haired Natalie, with her big brown eyes, stood next to her father holding her stuffed dolly.

Kate had been busy working in the store and taking care of their two small children and, of course, their sixty-eight-pound puppy named Moonies. Moonies went to the store every day with Kate, where he would lie under the counter as the store mascot.

Kate's parents were at the ribbon cutting, along with Christopher, her grandmother, and various friends. Marge, from the bakery, was bustling around and bringing over lots of pastries and other goodies.

As Kate cut the ribbon, her mother, Grace, snapped pictures. "Katie, smile," she'd say, taking picture after picture. Local store owners cheered her on. This had been a long time coming. Kate had worked in the store since it had opened.

The original owner was never there and everyone had already been referring to Beauty on Request as Kate's store. Now it finally was. It had taken an additional year to pay off the loan, but the store was finally theirs.

Tom was even more proud of his wife's accomplishment than she was. He loved everything about Kate, especially her determination to be successful. The store was constantly busy, because of her dedication and careful attention to her customers.

Things were going great for the Verdis. Tom had started his own business and had a beautiful office close to home. His business was expanding, as was their bank account. They were house hunting for a bigger place and finally starting to reap the rewards of their hard labor.

A few months after the reopening of the store, Tom and Kate were planning a trip to New York. They hadn't been back since before Tyler was born. Tom was in the bedroom, putting his things in a suitcase, when Kate walked in holding the real estate section of the newspaper.

"Tommy," she said sweetly, "there are some really beautiful homes in Thousand Oaks overlooking the mountains—and they're huge." She handed the newspaper to Tom.

"Wow, thirty-four-hundred square feet," he said, glancing over the newspaper. He read the real estate ad and said, "They're pretty expensive, though. I don't think we can afford anything like this."

"Yeah, well," she said, giving him a sultry look, "it says there's a two-way fireplace between the master bathroom and the bedroom."

"Yeah?" he said, smiling back at her.

"Yeah, well," Kate said, giggling, "you could be lying on the bed and watch me take my bath with the fireplace going."

"We can do that without the fireplace," Tom said facetiously.

"Yeah, but picture how much better I'll look with the fireplace going." Kate smiled at him and asked, "Can we just go look when we get back from New York? Please?"

Tom looked down at her through half-closed eyes and whispered, "Why don't you talk me into it?"

Kate walked over to the bedroom door, closed it, and locked it. Then she pulled off her T-shirt and did just that.

Boarding the plane was a different experience, now that Tom and Kate had two small children. She was carrying Tyler on her hip, her purse, toys, and baby paraphernalia. Tom had the carry-on bag, toys, and unneeded garbage while trying to hold Natalie's hand. It was quite an event, with the baby crying and Natalie misplacing her stuffed dolly.

"Thank God we found that doll," Kate said, sounding desperate. "The whole trip would have been a nightmare without it."

"Oh yeah, like it's not a nightmare now," Tom said, not amused with the trip so far. "My parents are gonna have to visit us next time. It's just a major pain in the ass to visit them with all this crap."

Kate looked at him and nodded in agreement.

The entire plane ride was a disaster. Tyler cried most of the time, while Natalie whined about how uncomfortable she was. Tom and Kate took turns trying to change Tyler's diaper, which they both insisted was the worst one they had ever seen.

Finally the plane landed and the passengers stood up to begin the deboarding process. Tom was behind Kate and the kids, trying to pull his carry-on bag out from the overhead compartment. He said a few choice words under his breath as he struggled with the suitcase, and a pretty, young woman standing next to him leaned over to help. When Tom glanced over at her, he was caught off guard by her sexiness—and the flirty look that she gave him. Kate was looking up front, caught up in the confusion of the other passengers trying to get off the plane, so she didn't notice a thing. Nothing happened. It was just one of those moments when two people's eye's meet, and you knew in an instant, that she was going to end up in Tom's bed—wearing the beret.

"Thank you," Tom said to the young woman, who just smiled. He was obviously with his family, but if he had been alone, she would have been glad to get to know him a whole lot better. He returned the sentiment with the thought, *You have no idea how much I wish I were single right now.* But then his mind wandered back toward reality and the fact that he loved his wife and kids.

The trip was not at all a vacation for Tom. He loved seeing his family and friends, but after a while, he was eager to go home. Home was now his warm bed in California. He had lived there long enough that it had become his home. Both his kids had been born in Thousand Oaks, and his job was there. Home had changed the way he thought about his life and what he wanted to accomplish. He had the desire to be successful now, a desire that hadn't existed before he married Kate.

Tom and Kate had borrowed his parents' van to take the kids for a drive down Main Street. Huge pots filled with colorful geraniums hung in the middle of the manicured median. It was memory lane for Kate, who was excited to be back in town, pointing out every special place where Mommy and Daddy had made their mark.

"Natalie, look, honey." Smiling, Kate pointed to the old pub on the corner. "That's Moonies, where Mommy and Daddy met. That's who Moonies, our doggie, is named after. I used to work there."

Natalie answered her mother in her little girl voice, not able to pronounce every word properly yet. "Dat's who our doggie's names atter, Mommy? Can we go inside?"

"It doesn't look like they're open right now. Maybe we'll come back later for a snack." Kate looked at Tom and said, "I wonder if Leonard is still the manager."

"Sure he is. Nothing changes in this town," Tom said. "You can come back in fifty years, and he'll have white hair and still be the manager."

Kate laughed. Looking out the window and enjoying happy memories, she said, "Oh honey, let's take the kids by the gym and show them where you coached."

Tom looked in his rearview mirror at Tyler sitting in his car seat. "Tyler, you wanna go see where Daddy worked?" Tyler just looked back with Kate's blue eyes and smiled, unsure of what his dad had said, but loving the sound of his voice. Without hesitation, Tom made a right turn into the parking lot of the school.

As Kate was getting the kids out of the van, Tom looked up at the building, his heart flooded with thousands of memories from when he had attended school there. Then he picked up Tyler and ran his fingers through his son's pale blond hair as if combing it. "Come on, Tyler boy. I'm gonna show you where Daddy used to play basketball."

Kate took Natalie's hand as Natalie held her stuffed dolly, and they all walked in as a family. The only one missing was Moonies, who was at home in California with Kate's brother, Christopher.

As they walked down the long hall, they saw a trophy case. Tom paused and said, "I wonder if it's still ... Yes, there it is."

"What, honey?" asked Kate.

Tom pointed to an old photo of himself holding a huge trophy. The caption underneath read, "Most Valuable Player four years in a row."

Kate stopped to look. She had seen the photo before, but she acted like she hadn't.

"Oh my gosh, honey. Look, kids, that's Daddy." She picked Natalie up, so she too could get a closer look at the picture.

Natalie pointed to the picture and said to her doll, "Look Lulu, there's

Daddy." Everyone stared in admiration at Tom, and Kate said, "Come on, hon, let's go show them the gym."

When they walked into the gym, a few guys were playing basketball. Several minutes later, one of the players—a tall young man with a goatee and spiked hair—noticed Tom. "Coach V? Hey, it's Coach V!" The young man came running toward Tom and his family. "Coach V, hey." He hugged Tom and then shook his hand.

It took Tom a minute, but then he realized who it was. "Mark? Oh my gosh, buddy! I didn't place you at first." Tom hugged the guy again and said, "Man, look at you. You look great. How've you been?"

Kate stood there smiling, thinking this must be someone with whom Tom had gone to high school. Tom introduced Mark to Kate, and then Mark called his girlfriend over from across the gym. A pretty, young, collegiate-looking girl walked over and was introduced as Mark's fiancée.

Mark started telling his girlfriend about a practice that he had had with Coach Tom years ago when he was in high school. The young man explained how, when he had tried to make a basket, he had slipped and everyone had fallen on top of him. Mark had ended up in the emergency room. He lifted his leg to show the young girl his battle scar from the accident.

Kate stood in disbelief. She remembered the incident perfectly, but this grown man seemed so different from the kid in that accident just a few short years ago. Had she changed that much? she wondered. She listened to the young man tell his fiancée what a great coach Tom was, and that Tom had been his inspiration to become a coach himself. Kate left the gym feeling even more proud of her wonderful husband.

Tom left the gymnasium realizing that he had outgrown coaching and Canandaigua. Life was too slow there. The homes were old, and the restaurants were simple and redundant. Everyone from his hometown seemed content with so little, but Tom wanted more out of life—and he knew that he could get it.

Tom was different now. He had adjusted to the fast-paced, opulent lifestyle of Los Angeles. He loved the variety of restaurants, the many huge shopping centers, and even the way people dressed. He liked not knowing everyone in town.

His trip to Canandaigua was enlightening. During their visit, Tom became increasingly self-confident and developed a clear vision of what he wanted to accomplish in life. His business was already strong, and he knew that with just a little more perseverance and dedication, it would grow to an even higher level. He had Kate—who was even more than the woman of his dreams—a daughter, and a son. Now Tom also had the vision to achieve things in life that previously had seemed impossible. He felt a burning power to conquer everything within his reach.

Why not? he thought. *Why not get that beautiful, gigantic home with the double fireplace?* He hadn't even seen it yet, but he already knew he wanted it. *Why not a Porsche someday?* Tom was beginning to think of such luxuries as things that he could obtain someday—and someday, he would.

As Tom's vision and dreams for the future became clear to him, his determination to obtain it powerfully transformed him. The small trip back home to Canandaigua changed Tom forever. He resolved to become the very best and achieve the perfect life—not realizing that he had already accomplished that.

"The kids had so much fun with your parents," Kate said, looking out the airplane window. "I love the way your dad could make Tyler laugh. I've never seen Tyler giggle like that before."

"Yeah, my folks look great," Tom said. "I can't wait to get home, though."

Kate agreed, "Yeah, home to our cozy bed."

They smiled at each other. Both kids were asleep, and the flight home was a lot easier than the flight to New York.

"Kate?" Tom said.

Her attention diverted from the plane window, Kate said, "Yeah?"

"Let's look at that house when we get back to Thousand Oaks."

"What house?"

"The house with the double fireplace," Tom said.

Kate's blue eyes widened, and her mouth opened. She couldn't believe her ears. She looked tired from the restless trip, but she was suddenly revived by his suggestion. "Tom, are you sure?"

"I'm not saying we're gonna get it," he said, suddenly realizing the magnitude of his remark. "Let's just go and look."

Kate replied, "Okay, okay. Oh!"

She was excited, and he knew that he was in for it. He might as well just write the check right then and there, he told himself.

The rest of the flight was quiet for both of them. They were individually fixated on what they were going to do when they arrived home. Tom sat there analyzing his business and how he was going to pay for such a house. Kate sat there trying to calculate just how she was going to decorate such a home.

Tom and Kate had an embellished vision culminating in the same dream—to buy a bigger, better home and make a tremendous amount of money. Each of them embarked on a quest to take their business to the top—Tom with T. Verdi and Associates, and Kate with Beauty on Request.

Seven

꧁ঔৣ꧂

The erotic music filled the dark nightclub, along with the warm, sweaty bodies throwing themselves around the floor to the slow, intense beat of the music. High up on the platform overlooking the dance floor, a pair of very high-heeled, patent-leather Dolce & Gabbana boots were dancing like a professional. Only a select few were permitted to dance on the exhibit platform—the extremely good-looking or the impeccably dressed. She was both.

Attached to the tight black boots were the long, lean, fabulously bare legs of Athena. Wrapped around her hips was a sheer gold and black Chanel scarf worn as a makeshift miniskirt. Her entirely bare midriff revealed a flat, tanned stomach with a tiny, jeweled belly button. Under the scarf were ribbons posing as panties and an ass that surpassed perfection. She was raw, salacious and glamorous—the Goddess.

Athena had a rock-hard body, and when she shook on the platform, nothing else on her body did unless she was in the mood to display her healthy cleavage. She danced slowly and seductively, like a Moroccan belly dancer. She shone radiantly through the mood and the atmosphere.

Athena glanced down at the crowd and noticed Dolphia, her Cuban bouncer friend, watching her dance. Athena's honey-colored hands, covered in shiny silver jewelry, were held on display above her head, intertwining and extending a clean, natural, no-polish manicure.

"You're staring again, Dolphia," she seductively yelled down to him.

"That's because you're so damn orgasmic, Athena," he yelled back, with an alluring grin on his face. His soft, boyish voice made it obvious he was gay.

"You would know," she answered erotically, and they both laughed.

They had indulged in each other's bodies a few times, although Dolphia was predominately homosexual. He had a lover of three years named Antonio, a gorgeous, dark Italian who had enjoyed Athena with Dolphia. She took pleasure in watching the two of them make love. Their beautiful, strong, mocha-colored bodies looked like something from a Greek painting. They displayed a different kind of affection for each other in lovemaking than men and women usually do—not because of the obvious reason, but because of how the two men indulged in each other. They devoured each other emotionally and physically, and they gave much more of themselves to each other than most straight lovers do. She was addicted to the powerful intensity that was present when the two men would climax, and she found it insanely alluring. They made lovemaking look like an art form.

Athena had almost turned Dolphia straight once or twice, or so she thought. She confused him with her playful but aggressive foreplay, a diversion from what he was used to with the guys. But Dolphia was in love with Antonio, and that was fine with Athena.

Dolphia was handsome and well built, but Athena wasn't interested in him in any way other than sexual gratification. She loved gaining knowledge about what men found sexually interesting in other men. She mastered a few tricks from Dolphia, and she was always eager to return the favor.

After several dances, she stepped down from the platform to greet Dolphia. "Hey, baby boy," she said as she put her soft hand underneath his chin and placed a delicate, friendly kiss on his lips.

"You are such a fucking goddess," he said with a laugh.

"Thus my name," she said conceitedly.

"It fucking fits you perfectly," he said, "although Athena should mean 'goddess of powerful seduction' rather than 'goddess of art and wisdom.'"

Athena gave him a flaunting suggestion of her bosom. "A goddess is a goddess, my love," she insisted.

Dolphia nodded in agreement.

Athena had arrived at the exclusive Miami nightclub alone, which was how she preferred it. She had enough confidence to go to a club, have a few drinks, and dance alone, merely to see the reaction of all who noticed her. She loved to mess with married men and guys who were there with their girlfriends. It was a cat and mouse game that she always found entertaining, and Dolphia would sometimes play along.

Dolphia said, "You look amazing, my little ghost orchid. Let me see you." He pulled both her hands above her head and spun her around. "If I wasn't gay—"

"You're not gay, remember?" joked Athena, cutting him off. It reminded them of a most satisfying evening, and they both laughed. "Let's get a martini," she suggested, and they walked over to the bar.

The club was famous for its DJ and alcoholic beverages that glowed in the dark with colored, mechanical ice cubes. "Where's Antonio?" Athena asked as she sipped her bright blue martini.

"He's at home sulking, as usual," Dolphia said, sipping his drink.

"Sulking? What the hell for?"

"He's pissed at me, because I moved the sofa toward the window."

"What the hell? He's pissed at you for that?" Athena stirred her martini with the olive stick. "So move it back," she said, offering an easy solution to the problem.

"Well, he's also pissed at me because"—Dolphia stalled before confessing—"I sold his coffee table."

Athena's eyes widened, and what had started as a sip of her drink turned into a gulp. "Shit! That table he got in Venice? Why would you do that?" she asked, obviously confused. "He loved that table. No wonder he's pissed at you."

"Oh well, missy," Dolphia said, "have you forgotten who he went to Venice with? Ohhhh, maybe was it … Daniel?"

"Oh, not that old shit story again," Athena said in an annoyed tone. "You two were broken up."

"I don't give a flying bull's ass," Dolphia said, getting upset at the thought of his current lover going on a trip with his ex. He continued, like a lawyer defending his case, "I don't want that fucking table in our home."

Athena rolled her eyes as she finished her drink. Then she ended the conversation, saying, "I'm gonna go dance and have some fun. You two work it out."

When Athena entered an establishment, it was only a matter of time before she had everyone's attention. She would glide into a club, usually in stiletto sandals. Her long bronze hair, with its golden streaks from the Florida sun, would glisten in the nightclub light, waving and flowing behind her like a national flag.

Always the same game, it never failed. There would be some guy in the club with a woman. At some point, he would notice Athena and make some excuse to his date to go to the bathroom, bar, whatever. He'd mingle into the crowd and then make his way around the bar toward Athena, offer to buy her a drink, and try to get her phone number. She'd always give him some bogus, bullshit number and leave the club amused, laughing to herself and feeling invincible. She knew she was a powerhouse, and she always used it to her advantage, such as getting jobs in places where she was paid more than she was worth.

Athena had been living in Florida for the past five years. She had arrived in the tropical city of Boca Raton in a limousine. All she had with her was a bronze silk bridesmaid's dress and a small purse with her driver's license and one credit card in it.

Within a few short days, she had managed to hook up with an old friend whom she and Joliet had visited regularly in the summer, and it wasn't long before Athena established a new life in Florida. It had been apparent at Joliet's wedding that she had to move on from her life in Chicago. Not that she was the type of girl who cared what anyone thought of her, but the scandal she had created was more than anyone could recover from.

Throughout her life, Athena had always possessed the self-confidence of a fire-breathing dragon. She was strong, focused, and not intimidated by anything. Her strength came from the survival instinct she had acquired from the pain she endured after her father left. The transformation she had felt take place deep in her soul came from the hatred she felt for the woman who had stolen her father away. That hate became a fascination that Athena couldn't ignore—a fascination that changed her from a sweet, loving little child into a methodical, calculating vixen, determined to be the temptress and never again the victim.

Athena had developed the moxie and determination to be the best at everything she did. She was always eager to impress anyone and everyone, no matter what she was participating in. Whether it was a school contest or collecting Girl Scout badges, Athena was always the best. She graduated from college at the top of her class and earned a master's degree in math. Eager to become independently wealthy, especially after seeing what money had afforded Joliet's family, she had already become bored with Chicago and was finding it to be a dead end.

Athena grew up with Joliet, but always felt like she was on the outside looking in. Joliet shared everything she had with her best friend, but Athena couldn't help feeling like a guest in Joliet's life. Athena considered Joliet to be her best and closest friend, but Athena couldn't stop resenting Joliet for having all the things she wanted.

Joliet had a mom, dad, and brother—a family, which Athena never had. The only person Athena really loved was her mother. After her father left,

Athena was devastated and heartbroken, and she couldn't let herself love another person. She managed to convert the love that she once had for her father into strength and power within herself.

She wasn't about to play second fiddle to Joliet's David. Athena had been friends with Joliet long before David came along. And once again, she felt like she was being replaced by someone else. Naturally, Joliet spent most of her time with David, and Athena felt Joliet slipping out of her life. She knew David was a great and gorgeous guy, but also just a typical guy in many ways—and therefore not worthy to be Joliet's love or replace Athena in Joliet's life.

She really didn't see what she had done to her best friend as *betrayal*, after having time to think about it during the long ride to Florida. After all, it was a travesty that David was getting married at all, since he obviously wanted to sleep with Joliet's best friend. Athena had known all along that David wanted to sleep with her, since the day he first met her. His curiosity proved her assumption to be right. He loved Joliet with his whole heart, but like most men, he was helpless in the presence of Athena.

Athena knew that Joliet and David's marriage would never have lasted. She insisted to herself, *I did them a favor. One day they'll see it my way.*

Early in her transition to Boca Raton, Athena accepted a job as a cocktail waitress at a posh and affluent golf resort. There she met a very wealthy and very married businessman who fell helplessly under Athena's charismatic spell. With their budding relationship, she developed a new strategy for earning income.

Her ploy was to find a successful businessman who was obviously dedicated to his family, and then lead him astray by making herself extremely interesting to him. She'd give him a few sexually enlightened months, which would get him wrapped around her little G-string finger. She'd then beg the man to leave his wife and children, knowing of course that he never would. He'd insist that he couldn't because of the children, so she'd pretend to be lonely, helpless, and even suicidal.

That first wealthy businessman, whom she had met at the Boca Raton golf resort, felt horrible over her grief, and he gave Athena two hundred thousand dollars to ease her pain. Athena skipped away happy, gave herself a pat on the back for a job well done, and headed for the nearest spa, where she spent the next two days being pampered. For a while after that, Athena didn't work. She did, however, buy a white convertible Corvette and a condo by the beach. Her time was spent going to clubs, mingling and doing things that most people wouldn't dream of doing.

Up on the block, dancing in the spotlight with her new $1,700 boots, Athena felt spectacular. Peering through half-closed eyes at the familiar patrons beneath her, she was powerful. Young and hip, she knew who she was, and she knew she had it going on, all over the people below her. Even if most of them had more money than she did, she possessed a gift that none of them had. Athena had the power of influence, and that was worth more than any fortune they could acquire.

Over the past few months, Athena had pondered the idea of moving to another city. She was beginning to feel a desire to move on, like there was something else waiting for her out there. She loved Boca, she thought to herself as she danced. She might even retire there one day, although the idea of retirement made her laugh. But for now she was done with Florida. It was time for new surroundings and new faces.

On previous occasions, she had toyed with the idea of relocating. But now, on the platform and dancing hard to the music, the idea seemed to rush through her body and grab hold of her, as if it were something that had to be done, maybe even as soon as the following day. She felt a thrill as she started to dance even more erotically, knowing that tomorrow would bring a new sunset to the end of her day and a new horizon to the beginning of her new life.

The next afternoon, Athena was lying on her stomach in a lounge chair at the community pool. Her right leg was bent upward, with her red polished toes pointing to the sky. She was wearing a white thong bikini, and her top strap was undone so that she wouldn't have tan lines. Her hair was in a ponytail, high on her head. Nearby sunbathers were looking at her in envy.

Reading through dark sunglasses, she studied an assortment of travel magazines and brochures, trying to decide where to go next. She toyed with the idea of Boston, Massachusetts, but she preferred to go somewhere she hadn't been before. Las Vegas was a definite possibility. Then she came across a brochure for a new resort in Santa Barbara, California, that she found very appealing. The Bacara Resort and Spa had special treatments that Athena was familiar with, and the hotel was on the ocean, which was also appealing.

She sat up, leaving her straps hanging, and reached into the leather case next to her lounge chair. As she pulled out her laptop, the obvious tan lines of the tiny triangles that covered her nipples were exposed, leaving nothing to the imagination of the old man across from her. Athena was curious about the hotel and its management—and oblivious to the elderly couple sitting across from her. The irritated wife was sneering, while the man was thrilled with the unexpected entertainment.

Done with the sun, she tied up her top. Lazing around the pool had become secondary to finding her new destination. "This looks like a great place," she said as she circled the information about the Santa Barbara resort with a pencil. She got out her cell phone and made a call to the resort, asking for information about the hotel.

The older woman sitting with her husband was boiling mad at Athena's lack of modesty. She nudged her husband and said, "Come on. Let's go." As they started to walk away, she glared at Athena and remarked, "Young women these days have no shame." The man grabbed his towel and followed his wife, but didn't say a word.

Athena never saw them. She was too interested in what she was doing to notice anything going on around her. She just immersed herself in her computer, looking for the next place she could call home.

She got the information she needed about the management, so she could do a little homework on it. But she knew better than to submit a résumé and risk being rejected. Instead, she made a plan to move to Santa Barbara, confident that she would get the job. She knew she had to investigate the situation, but there was no question that her personal presentation would seal the deal. The more she learned about Santa Barbara, the more enthusiastic she became about moving there.

When Athena finished her research, she sorted things out in her mind. There wasn't much she needed to do before moving. She would put her condo up for sale in the morning and have her things sent to California. She would either drive or sell the Corvette and fly. *Minor details*, she thought to herself.

By the end of the day, Athena had made up her mind and decided on her destination. She didn't know what the future held, but she was excited to embark on a fresh new life full of fun and excitement. She decided to put most her things up for sale and buy everything she needed when she got there. She wanted a new car, a new place, and maybe even a new man. Athena was about to reinvent herself once again—in California.

Eight

On an early summer morning, the doorbell rang at the Verdi house. It was three men from the moving company, ready to take the family's belongings to their beautiful new home. The living room was obviously in transition. Everything was packed and ready for the move.

Kate came running downstairs wearing a gray sweat suit, and a small white towel rested on her shoulder. She met Tom in the entryway, where he held his morning cup of coffee. He was wearing a sleeveless T-shirt that revealed his impressive arms. Tom and Kate were almost too excited to breathe.

"Good morning, Mr. Verdi, Mrs. Verdi," one of the movers said.

"Good morning," Tom and Kate greeted them simultaneously.

The man said, "We're from Alpert's Moving Company."

"Yes, come in," Tom said.

"Is everything going?" the man asked.

Tom looked at Kate for the answer. "Everything except those couches," she said. "We're having new couches delivered to our new home tomorrow."

Tom looked back at the movers with a pleased look and said, "My wife is just a little excited."

"Oh, like you're not," she said, joking back at him.

Tom put his arm around his wife and indicated to the movers, "Let us know if you need anything. We'll be in the kitchen packing the last-minute things."

"Would any of you like some coffee?" Kate offered.

"No, we just had breakfast. But thank you," said one of the movers. "We'll get started upstairs, okay?"

"That would be great," Kate said, "Our kids are at my mom's, so don't be afraid to go in their room." Then she followed Tom into the kitchen.

The rest of the day was exhausting for Tom and Kate. The early morning was spent moving their things out of their small condo and cleaning it for the new owners. The latter part of the day was spent organizing things in their beautiful new dream home, although moving from their small place to the triple-size home left the new house appearing sparse.

Kate looked around and commented, "The house looks bare, huh?"

"Well, the couches are coming tomorrow," Tom said. "Maybe next month we can buy a few more things."

Kate smiled at Tom and said, "Yeah, I can't wait to see how the new couches look in here. It's going to be so pretty." She looked tired, but her light blond hair and California smile were still attractive to Tom. They flirted with each other as they admired their new home and continued working to get things organized

With the exception of a short dinner break, the two stayed up until the wee hours of the morning, decorating what they started calling their new palace. The foyer floors were dark plank wood, which extended into the kitchen and most of the ground floor. There was also an elegant chandelier with an abundance of crystals hanging above the entryway. Most of the colors of the home were pale golds, dark and light greens, with touches of black. The home was gorgeous, and Tom and Kate were ecstatic.

It was about two in the morning when Tom realized that his wife had sneaked upstairs. He yelled up to her, "Kate! Katie!" When she didn't answer, he decided it was time to call it a day and get some sleep. He started up the staircase, but stopped to take a look around. He could smell the newness of the home, and he couldn't help but feel proud of what he and Kate had accomplished. They had been married only five and a half years, and already they had two beautiful children and this gorgeous new home. He felt so happy. Tom had never dreamed that he could have such a full life. He remembered the house in New York he had grown up in. Although it had been filled with love, that house was small, quaint, and nothing of this magnitude. He had definitely hit the jackpot, Tom thought to himself, and he felt like a king.

Tom continued up the stairs, tired and ready to go to bed. He walked through the double doors that opened into his new bedroom and was surprised that the fireplace was lit. Through the two-sided fireplace, he saw that Kate had slipped into the bathtub and was enjoying her new bathroom. The lights were off, and several lit candles were placed around the tub. Kate's pale blond hair was piled on top of her head and her beautiful luminous face was seductive.

She said softly, "The kids are at my parents' house, Tom. Let's take advantage of it. Take your clothes off and get in here with me."

He was interested, but really tired. "Aren't you tired, babe? We've been working all day."

Kate looked down at the tub filled with bubbles and then back up at Tom with a seductive grin on her face. She lifted her body slightly, raising her nipples above the bubbles, and looked at him with her big blue eyes. "Please?"

She was irresistible to Tom as he felt his hard-on emerging. He pulled off the T-shirt he had been wearing, exposing his strong, muscular torso, and unbuttoned his jeans. He slipped them down, causing his tight black briefs to go along with them. Kate's excitement was evident as she stared at his big, hard, beautiful cock.

Tom stepped into the tub and knelt down on top of her. He kissed her on her mouth as he brought her up closer to him, getting between her legs. With one hand, he directed his throbbing hard penis and pushed it in. He began fucking Kate slowly, causing the water to splash over the sides of the tub.

Both Tom and Kate were too caught up in the excitement of their new home and the passion of their fucking to care about the water on the floor. They spent the next few moments christening their new home.

Two months later, the Verdis decided to have their family and friends over for a housewarming. The wonderful little party gave Kate an opportunity to show off her cooking skills. She served special appetizers and desserts that she had been preparing all week. Everyone was amazed at how fast Tom and Kate had pulled the house together and how spectacular it looked.

Grace, Kate's mother, entertained Natalie and Tyler while Kate hustled around in the kitchen. Moonies rested quietly in front of the fireplace. Everyone was either touring the home, munching on goodies, or talking about how great Tom and Kate looked. The Verdis had it going on, and it was obvious to everyone that they had it all.

Cynthia Reyes walked into the kitchen after finishing a tour of the home. She had been Kate's best friend since junior high school. "Katie, your house looks almost as awesome as you do," she said. Then she took a breaded zucchini from the appetizer plate Kate was preparing, took a bite, and swooned. "Ahh, these are fucking great," she whispered.

Cynthia was athletic-looking, with light brown hair and a sassy personality. She was in the middle of her second divorce, but still maintained a healthy outlook on relationships. "I love, *love* this house. I'm moving in with you guys. I'll take the downstairs bedroom, right next to the bar," she joked, with a devilish grin on her face. She sipped her tequila and they laughed. Then Cynthia gave her friend a once-over and said, "Katie, you look amazing in that dress."

Kate looked down at her dark red, perfectly tight-fitting dress and answered with a matching grin, "You can move in anytime, as long as you babysit."

Cynthia smiled and kept munching on the goodies. "I'm serious—you look magnificent. What have you been doing to yourself? I mean, is the sex really that goddamn great?"

Kate said, "It sure the hell is." She giggled, but then said in a more serious tone, "But I'm happy. I'm just so happy. Tom is the perfect guy for me, and we have this perfect thing going." Her eyes wandered around the room until they found Tom. "I just never imagined I would ever have such a great thing going, but I do." Then she looked at Cynthia and giggled again, adding, "And yes, the sex is off the fucking charts. *Great!*"

Cynthia shook her head and said, "Well, it shows. It definitely shows. I've never seen you look this great, not even in high school. I wish someone would pump me like that."

They giggled and toasted each other with their cocktails, but they were interrupted by the screaming voice of Tyler being chased by Natalie.

"Gimme back my dolly, Tyer," Natalie yelled.

Tyler screamed, "No!"

"Give her back to me, Tyer!" Natalie yelled again.

Kate tried to intervene. "Tyler give Lulu back to Natalie now!"

Tyler tried to get away with the doll, but he ran right into Cynthia's knees.

Cynthia said with a smile, "Hey, just a minute, fella. I usually get dinner first." When Kate laughed, Cynthia glanced up at her and said underneath her breath, "Well, not always." They both laughed more. Then Cynthia took the doll and asked gently, "Can I have this, please?" Tyler started to turn away. "Hey, wait," Cynthia said. "Can I have a hug first?" He ran back, hugged her, and then ran into the other room.

Kate was temporarily irritated by her children. She was bustling around from one counter to the next, getting more appetizers for the guests. "I don't know what it is lately, but in the past month, those two have been arguing so much. It's so friggin' irritating."

Cynthia came to their defense. "Oh, it's just because you've been working so hard on this house. They're adorable, Kate. They really are."

Kate answered, somewhat facetiously, "Oh yeah, they're charming."

"No, really, Kate," Cynthia said. "Some kids are a pain in the ass, but yours are so damn cute. I love Nat's voice and the way she tries to say Tyler's name. *Tyer*—it's so precious."

"You're biased," Kate said with a chuckle.

"Well, yes, I am. But what do you expect? You're just their mother, but I'm their godmother. There's a big difference." Cynthia paused as she put a small carrot in her mouth and chewed it down. "Besides, they're probably the only kids I'll ever have."

Kate looked at her with a confused look and asked, "Haven't you heard from Bill?"

"That fuckface? No. I told you, didn't I, that he took Belinda on a cruise?"

Kate's eyes widened in disbelief. "No!"

"Yeah, so we're never mentioning that asshole again," Cynthia said. "He's worse than both my ex-husbands put together." She shoved a small mushroom in her mouth as Kate shook her head and laughed.

Just then Grace walked in the kitchen and asked, "Do you need any help, dear?"

Kate answered, "Oh, no, Mom. I was just refilling the veggie plate. Does it seem like everyone's having a good time?"

"Yes," her mother said, "everyone's having a ball. Your father's out there telling his jokes."

Kate looked at Cynthia and said, "Uh-oh." Just then they heard the crowd in the living room burst out in laughter, and Kate said, "Oh, okay" with a sigh of relief.

She then took a bone out of the freezer and said jokingly, as she walked over to Moonies, "I have to give this to my other son." She persuaded Moonies to follow her out into the garage, where she gave him the bone.

When the housewarming party was over, the Verdi home was filled with plants left by their guests. Tom and Kate retreated upstairs to their bedroom. Tom carried Natalie asleep on his shoulder, and Kate carried Tyler asleep on hers. Moonies fell asleep in front of the fireplace, stuffed from all the goodies he had been fed throughout the evening. The Verdis fell asleep, happy in their new home.

Nine

❧⧉☙

Kate awoke to a warm beam of light resting on her face and the sweet sound of birds chirping at her window. She smiled when she realized that she and Tom had been married exactly seven years. She leaned over to look at the clock. It was 6:17 in the morning and there was no sight of Tom, so she assumed that he was in the bathroom

"Tom," she whispered softly. "Tom?" When he didn't respond, she tried again a little louder, but careful not to wake the kids. "Tom!" He still didn't answer, so she got out of bed and grabbed her robe to cover her short nightie. She peeked in Tyler's room to find him still asleep. Then she went to Natalie's room, where she too was sleeping, and Moonies was resting in front of her bed.

As Kate approached the staircase, she could smell the aroma of bacon cooking and hear someone moving around in the kitchen. She walked down the stairs and through the hallway, careful not to make any noise so that she could sneak up on her husband.

When she got to the kitchen, Kate giggled, unable to keep her composure. She was pleasantly surprised to see Tom scrambling eggs with his back toward her, completely naked and wearing her faux-mink apron. She thought it was sweet and adorable that he was standing there wearing a woman's apron with his butt exposed for her enjoyment.

Tom was cooking a spectacular breakfast for their anniversary. And to show that he hadn't lost his sex appeal and silliness, he was cooking in the buff. With obvious approval, Kate said, "Now *this* is my kind of restaurant."

In a French accent, he asked, "You like?"

"Yes," she answered, "as a matter of fact, I like very much."

Tom walked over and gave her a gentle kiss while holding the spatula. "Happy anniversary, babe," he said.

"Happy anniversary, Tom," Kate said adoringly. "I love you so much."

He answered her in a sweet, chipper voice, "I love you."

Then Kate asked with a smile and eyebrows raised, "What would you have said if one of the kids had come downstairs first?"

"I don't know," he answered. "Trick or treat?"

She snuggled into his apron and said, "Yeah, well, I'll take this treat." Then she reached underneath his apron and grabbed his goodie bag. They both laughed and she whispered into his ear, "I want this huge sausage with my breakfast."

"Em, hem?" he questioned with a smile.

Kate walked over to the stove and looked at the delicious breakfast being prepared.

"Oh my God, Tom, this looks fantastic. Forget it. I'm starving."

He laughed and said, "I knew you'd love this." He picked up a plate full of food and brought it over to the table. "Here, sit down. This is yours." Then he walked over to the refrigerator, got two elegant glasses filled with champagne, and handed one to her.

Tom stood there in his apron, his dark-brown eyes staring into hers. "Here's to the best seven years of my life. And to you, the woman who's given me the best sex I could ever dream of."

Kate laughed. She knew that Tom was joking, but she loved how he could be so sexual about everything. She kissed him and then they enjoyed their breakfast as they reminisced about the past seven years they'd spent together.

When they were just about finished with breakfast, Tom casually said to Kate, "After you finish your coffee, why don't you get dressed and we'll go look at those Range Rovers you've been talking about."

Kate put her fork down and looked at him in disbelief. "Oh my God, Tom, are you kidding?" she asked. She threw her arms around him and shrieked with ecstasy.

Tom smiled and said, "We can go take a look. I got the Kestler account last week. I was gonna tell you, but then I thought I might surprise you with this."

Obviously elated, Kate said, "Surprise me? I can't believe we're gonna look at Range Rovers." She sounded like a child at Christmas. "I've wanted one since before I met you."

"Well, we'll see how much they are, and maybe"—Tom paused—"we *might* be able to get one."

"Oh, yay!" Kate was bouncing around the room like a little kid.

That evening, Tom and Kate were getting ready to go to dinner and celebrate their anniversary. Kate was upstairs getting dressed when the doorbell rang. It was the babysitter, Lorraine, a teenager from up the street.

"Hi, Mr. Verdi," said the short-haired blond girl.

"Hi, Lorraine," Tom said as he let Lorraine in. "Thanks for babysitting tonight."

As she walked in and dropped her backpack by the sofa, Lorraine said, "Oh, no problem. I love babysitting Nat and Tyler. They're so cute." She paused and then asked, "Hey, did you guys get a new Range Rover?"

"Yeah, Kate's anniversary present," Tom said with a smile.

Lorraine said, "Wow, I love Range Rovers. They're so cool. My parents wanted one. They got a Nav instead, but I like Rovers better."

"Well, Kate deserved it," Tom said. "She's been working hard at the store and they've been doing real well over there, so I figured what the heck. You only live once, right?"

Lorraine replied, "Yeah."

Tom looked up the stairs and then back at Lorraine. "Hey, do me a favor, Lorraine. When Kate comes downstairs, keep her occupied, will you? I have a little present that I want to put in the car before she comes down." Looking upstairs again to make sure Kate wasn't listening, he said, "The kids are in the den watching television with Moonies."

Lorraine replied, "Oh, okay."

Tom sneaked out of the room to put his gift for Kate in the new car, and Lorraine went in the den to greet the kids.

A few minutes later, Kate walked down the stairs looking radiant. She was wearing a short, green, chiffon halter dress. Her legs were bare, her short boots were black and high-heeled, and her hair was pulled up loosely on top of her head.

"Wow," Tom said as he reentered the room, "you look amazing."

Just then Lorraine and the children walked in and joined in the compliments. "Oh, you do, Mrs. Verdi. You look beautiful," Lorraine said enthusiastically. Tyler added, in his baby voice, "You look bewiful, Mommy," not able to pronounce the words quite right. Natalie just stared at her mother.

Kate put her hand under her adoring daughter's chin and said, "Thank you, guys." Then she turned to Tom and said, "You look great too, Tom."

Tom smiled at his wife and said, "Let's go. We don't want to miss our reservation."

Kate walked over to the chair to get her coat and purse. "We won't be back late," she assured Lorraine.

Tom added, "Yes, we will. It's our one night out to party." Kate raised her eyebrows with a smile.

They walked outside to their new black Range Rover, and Tom opened the car door for Kate. The tan interior had the unmistakable smell of brand new leather.

Kate said happily, "Oh, it smells so wonderfully new in here. I love it."

When Tom got in, a hint of manly cologne followed him.

"You smell great, honey," Kate said. "I love that black shirt on you. It makes you look so sexy."

Tom looked at Kate and decided to go ahead and give her the surprise gift. He reached behind the seat and lifted up a large box the size of a basketball. It was wrapped in white paper with a big white bow on top. Tom leaned into Kate, and she could feel his breath as he spoke. "I was going to wait and give you this after dinner, but I can't wait. I want to give it to you right now."

"What the heck, Tom? I thought the Range Rover was my present."

"I didn't know we were going to get the car until I got that account," Tom explained. "But I had this made for you weeks ago, Kate. This is your real present, so open it up. You're gonna love it."

"I hate to break this to you, honey, but I'm not going to love anything more than I love this car," Kate said jokingly, "except maybe you." She smiled at him adoringly as she messed with the box. "What's in here? A deep fryer? This thing is huge."

Tom answered with a smile, "Yeah, I know, but quit talking about my dick and open the present."

Kate giggled and started to open the box.

Then Tom said with anticipation, "You're gonna freak out."

Kate took the paper off and saw a beautiful red velvet box. She looked at Tom more seriously and said, "What a beautiful box. What's inside?"

"Now you have to close your eyes," Tom said. "It's heavy, so I'll take it out. I want to hand it to you. Close your eyes."

Kate closed her eyes as Tom took the box from her. She could hear him fussing with the box, and a few moments later he said, "Okay, open your eyes."

He had turned the lights off so that it was dark inside the car. When Kate opened her eyes, the light coming from the glass globe in front of her was stunning. She saw her gift and gasped. As she looked at the large, glowing snow globe, tears welled up in her eyes.

Tom said, "I had it made for you, Kate. It's a snow globe with a night-light." Inside the snow globe was a miniature version of the night Tom and Kate fell in love. "See," he said, "that's us making the snow angels." There were two miniature people lying in the snow, smiling and making snow angels. "And see, that's us in my truck." He pointed to a miniature gray truck in front of the lake. Inside the truck were two people holding white Styrofoam cups and covered with a tiny red-plaid blanket.

"I can't believe this," Kate said, staring motionless at her gift.

Tom kept smiling and showing her every detail, realizing that he had given her the perfect gift. The snow globe was a perfect replica of that night. He pointed to the inscription, on a small metal band across the base of the snow globe, that read, "For the moment I'll never forget." Then he looked at Kate and said, "Are you ready for the best part?"

"What?" Her voice cracked, and she could barely get the words out. "There's more?"

Tom shook the globe so that the snow inside the glass ball was falling on the tiny lake. Then he rotated the base and a melody began playing. Tears streamed down Kate face as the voice of Dean Martin came softly from the globe, just as it had that night.

"Oh, my God," she said. "Tom, I can't believe it." He could barely understand her as she cried and threw her arms around him. "This is the most beautiful gift anyone has ever given anyone. I love you so much."

Tom lifted Kate's chin to tell her how he felt. As he looked deep into her eyes, he said, "When I was a kid growing up in Canandaigua, every once in a while, when I was playing or something, I would catch a look at the lake. Even as a kid, I knew it was the most beautiful thing in the world. As I got older, I was convinced that nothing was ever as pretty as that lake. But that night when we sat in my truck, I looked into your amazing blue eyes and realized that I had finally found something even more beautiful." He stared into Kate's tear-filled eyes and said, "Your eyes are the most beautiful things I've ever seen in this world, and I will never forget the moment when I realized that." Tom's eyes welled up with tears as he said, "I love you, Kate, more than anything in this world. I will always love you most of all."

Kate was out of control with emotion and tears. After seven years of marriage, they had more love for each other than ever before. They held each other for a private moment and then drove down to the beach, where they enjoyed a romantic dinner. Afterward they strolled alongside the ocean—barefoot, holding hands, and talking about their dreams for the future.

Later that night, after Lorraine had left and the kids were in bed, Kate was downstairs alone in front of the fireplace staring at her snow globe. She had placed it at the center of the fireplace mantel and was playing the Dean Martin melody.

Kate felt incredible, and she thought she was the luckiest woman in the world. She reminisced about the walk along the shore that she and Tom had taken earlier that night, and how lucky she was to have found her soul mate. She thought about her children nestled in their beds upstairs, and how life couldn't be any more perfect. When Dean Martin stopped playing from her snow globe, she turned the light off in the den and headed to bed.

When Kate reached the top of the stairs, she looked down into her living room with contentment. She thought to herself, *I love my life. I just love it.*

Ten

❧〜❧

Only fifty miles down the pacific coast, the captivating Goddess was skipping barefoot along the Santa Barbara shoreline, taunting the man following behind her. Bob Hayes, an overly zealous enthusiast, wanted to make Athena feel welcome in her new environment, so he had invited her out to dinner at the Balata Boat. Afterward, he carried her sandals while she enjoyed the beach in the early morning moonlight.

"Oh man," Athena yelled, "I love the water. I fucking love it here!"

"It's something, ain't it?" Bob said.

"Nothing can beat the beach in Santa Barbara," she yelled back, looking up at the sky. "Nothing on this planet!" The beaches in Florida were definitely spectacular, but there was something about the warm, dry air of California that Athena loved.

Bob strolled behind her, enjoying the shape of her legs and excited just to be in her presence. Bob had worked at the Bacara Resort in Santa Barbara since it opened three years earlier. He was the spa captain and worked as a fitness trainer in his spare time. Never married, Bob was in the market for a wife.

Athena was looking for a job when she met Bob. She had applied for a position as night manager and been unexpectedly turned down. When she was turned down a second time, Bob, who had a receding hairline and looked much older than his forty-one years, had come waltzing around the corner and introduced himself. He wasn't her type, but maybe he could be an avenue to employment in the hotel. Athena was always analytical about the people she met. She peeled people like onions, looking for any asset they might possess that could possibly advance her in some way.

Bob had tried to impress her by flaunting his title, which was mediocre at best. But he did come through in getting her an accounting job, which wasn't difficult given her math skills. Athena wasn't thrilled with the position. She wanted the more prestigious job as night manager, but she took the job as assistant accountant in hope that she could climb the ladder from there. Once again, Athena obtained what she wanted through her charms. Then she returned Bob's favor by accepting his dinner invitation.

Athena was holding up the sides of her sundress as she ran back and forth—enjoying the ocean surf, laughing, having a great time, and oblivious to anything Bob was doing. She said, in her mesmerizing way, "I am so turned on by California. I dig the ocean, and I love the moonlight on this sexy beach."

"You're a foxy little one, aren't you?" Bob said as he tried unsuccessfully to grab her hand.

"Bob, I like you," Athena said, "but I'm not interested in you that way. I'm sorry, Bob." He couldn't hide the disappointed look on his face as she continued, "I'm so glad I went to dinner with you, Bob. I'm having such a blast."

"I told you that you'd have a great time," he said, "Big Bob always comes through." The name *Big Bob* had been given to him by the more fit trainers at the resort because of his protruding belly. His coworkers would tease him about it from time to time.

Athena patted his tummy with kind intentions and said, "I love Santa Barbara. It's better than Boca and a hell of a lot better than snowbound Chicago."

"You didn't like living in Chicago?" Bob asked.

"I like Chicago," she said, "but I guess that since I grew up there, I'm tired of it." Running into the surf, she yelled, "But I love wearing little sundresses and cute sandals!" Bob just laughed.

They stayed a few more minutes, and then Athena said, "You know, I hate to lock down anything fun. But I'm working tomorrow at eleven, and it's gotta be past three." Bob looked back at the ocean and agreed. Then Athena asked, "You're working too, aren't you, Bob?"

"Yeah," he said, "I'm working the spa and fitness center at six o'clock tomorrow morning."

"Shit! Why didn't you say something? Let's go." Athena took her high-heeled sandals from him, and they started to walk along the beach and back up to the restaurant. "I'm working out tomorrow, Bob, so maybe I'll see you there," she said with an enchanting smile. "You can give me some pointers."

"Yeah, sure," Bob said. "What do you wanna work out?"

Athena lifted the side of her sundress, exposing a completely bare leg up to her waist. She was aware that in the dark where Bob was standing, it appeared that she was without panties. His mouth dropped in surprise at her risque gesture.

She said coyly, "I want to work *this* out." Then she slapped her backside, as if she didn't already have Bob's full attention. "I want to get this really hard."

He stared in disbelief as she ran the short distance back to the restaurant. Nothing else was said. Athena knew that she had planted the seed in Bob's head. Being the gossiper he was, it was only a matter of hours before every guy in the club heard what a fantastic ass Athena had. And she loved the attention that would undoubtedly get her.

The next afternoon, Bob was in the fitness center with an older, wealthier client named June O'Reily Blyermen. She was a petite woman in her early eighties, with short white hair, an Irish accent, and a frail, shaky voice. June worked out at the fitness center only for the social aspect of it—and because she enjoyed Bob's humor. She had hired him as her personal trainer after they met one afternoon during one of her many massage therapy sessions. Bob reminded June of the son she never had. She had been widowed and alone for more than twelve years, and she'd bounce back and forth between Palm Springs, Vegas, and Santa Barbara, staying a month at a time at each place.

"Now Junie," Bob said endearingly, "this next exercise is really going to tighten the tummy." June was listening seriously. "I know what you're thinking, Junie. You can tell that I do these exercises all the time," he said, rubbing his protruding stomach. "My svelte physique is probably intimidating to you. But remember, I'm a fitness trainer, so don't get discouraged."

June looked at him for a moment, took a second look, and then burst into laughter. "Oh, you silly Bobby. You're such a hoot," she said in her delicate old voice.

Smiling, he asked, "Why does everyone burst out laughing when I say that? I don't get it." Bob knew darn well that he didn't have the typical look of a trainer, but he had the charm to compensate for it.

Bob was coaching June on her exercise program, making sure she was doing everything correctly, when he felt someone pinch his butt. He turned around and was surprised to see Athena standing behind him. She was dressed in very short, tight, hip-hugger bike shorts, with a matching olive-green bra top and her dark red hair in a ponytail.

"Hey," he said, checking out her body, "I didn't think you'd make it."

Athena said, "What do you mean? Of course I made it."

"Well, we were on the beach so late last night that I didn't think you'd be up to it," Bob said.

"Big deal, I'm used to staying up late. I lived in Boca, remember?" Athena said. "Besides I'm only twenty-six, so I don't need much sleep."

June sat up and interrupted their conversation. She glanced over and noticed the beautiful young lady talking to Bob. "Bobby, go take your friend and get a root beer," she said in her delicate, shaky voice. "Go ahead. I can do these exercises by myself. Go with your girlfriend."

Bob raised his eyebrows at Athena, and she smiled. He wished he could say Athena was his girlfriend, but he knew otherwise and had to explain that to June. "June, this isn't my girlfriend. This is Athena Martine, who works here in the accounting department. She's new. Athena, this is June."

"Oh dear, I'm sorry," June said. "I hope I didn't embarrass the two of you." She turned to Athena and added, "Don't let a little old lady like me ruin things, dear."

Athena flashed a flawless white grin and gave June a little hug. "Oh no, really, you didn't ruin anything. We really are just friends."

June took Athena's hand between her own tiny, arthritic old hands. When she did so, she noticed Athena's watch and commented on it. "Oh, what a lovely watch, dear. A Cartier. Was it a gift, dear?"

"No," Athena answered. "I bought it myself when I lived in Boca Raton."

"Oh, you spent a pretty penny on that." June patted Athena's hand and held it a second longer. "It's a beauty, dearie, and it's so nice to meet you."

"Well, it's nice to meet you, June," Athena said in her youthful, sultry voice.

Meanwhile Bob was studying Athena's shorts, which fit her body like a latex glove and exposed a fascinatingly flat stomach. He said to her, "Man, only you could get away with those shorts."

"What do you mean?" Athena asked, but she knew exactly what he meant.

"I'm serious," Bob said. "I have belts wider than those shorts. Don't get me wrong—there's probably no one else on earth who would look that hot in that outfit."

As Athena turned to look at one of the machines, Bob could see the back of her shorts, perfectly outlining her butt and revealing an amazingly shaped derrière. "You don't have a lick of fat on you," he said. Then he went on about how tight Athena's stomach was and how strong her legs looked.

This wasn't new information to Athena, but she always enjoyed getting a good compliment. She just shrugged and got on with her workout.

Later that afternoon, Athena was busy working in the accounting office with her supervisor, Yolanda Valdez. The two women worked closely together in a small room with adjoining desks. Yolanda was a stout woman in her late fifties, with short wavy hair graying at the temples. She had come to America from San Salvador and worked at cleaning houses for seventeen years. She had saved up enough money to put herself through school and earned a bachelor's degree in accounting. She and her husband had one son, who lived in Santa Fe, where he had earlier attended college.

Athena was becoming familiar with the resort quickly and finding it a breeze to get through her assigned work. She was in the middle of a financial report when she broke the tip of her pencil and leaned over to get the sharpener. In doing so, she caught a glimpse of a photo on Yolanda's desk. "Is that you in that picture, Yolanda?" Athena asked.

"Yes, that's me," Yolanda answered, "and that's my husband, Bert." She pointed to a short, thin man with gray hair and a mustache. "We're at the Verdi housewarming party," she added, smiling at the picture of a group of obviously happy people.

"Looks like a friendly group," Athena said. Trying to sound more interested than she really was, she asked, "Are they relatives of yours?"

"No," Yolanda answered, but then paused and smiled. "Well, they're almost like relatives. We adore them just the same. About five or six years ago, when Bert was still an accountant, he helped Tom get started in the business. Now Tom's very successful and has a large book." Yolanda kept her eyes on her work as she continued to talk. "He's done very well for himself, and his wife, Kate, is spectacular." She picked up the frame and pointed to the good-looking couple who had their arms wrapped around their guests. "Here, see? This is them. Kate is the most beautiful woman you'll ever meet," Yolanda said proudly of her friend.

Athena glanced at Yolanda with a look of doubt, then looked back down at the picture, unimpressed with Kate's beauty.

"No, she really is beautiful—and charming," Yolanda insisted, sensing Athena's disbelief. "I've never met anyone like Kate. She's just amazing."

Athena asked, "Amazing in what way?"

"She's just a gorgeous and talented woman. Her hair is this luminous, pale blond—"

"Everyone in California has blond hair," Athena said, interrupting her.

Yolanda continued, "Her skin is like peaches and cream." Meanwhile the skepticism on Athena's face suggested that she would need more proof of Kate's spectacular nature. "The way she has decorated her home and the fabulous parties she throws," Yolanda said. "She's so involved with her children, and she still finds time to work in her store."

Athena asked, "What kind of store does she have?"

"A beauty supply store."

"Well, there you have it. That's why her skin looks like peaches and cream."

Yolanda shook her head and said, "You would just have to meet Kate, and then you would know what I mean. Katie is truly genuine, a beautiful person inside and out."

Athena said, "I guess."

"And they are just so in love with each other," Yolanda continued. "I've never seen a couple more in love."

Unable to hide her annoyed reaction, Athena said, "Oh brother."

Yolanda ignored her comment. Pausing for a moment to use her calculator, she then said, "And every time Tom looks at her, it's like he's seeing her for the first time. I've never seen a man more in love with a woman than Tom is with Kate."

Athena said, with a smirk, "Well, keep enjoying it, because even the peachiest of peaches get stale. He'll be looking for some fresh peaches and cream when they do."

"No, not a chance. Tom would never in a million years stray from Kate. He loves her too much, and he's just not that kind of guy."

Athena gasped in frustration. "Oh my God, you've got to be kidding me! They're *all* that kind of guy. If he's got a dick, he's that kind of guy. Even if he *doesn't* have a dick, he'll steal one from some other guy and *become* that kind of guy."

They both laughed, although Yolanda was struck by Athena's crass language. Yolanda was used to the way the younger people at the resort spoke, although she never took part in any of it. She had been raised to speak like a lady, and she never used profanity.

In a softer voice, Yolanda said, "I know what you're saying, but you'd just have to know the Verdis to understand what I mean." With that, she gave up and stopped trying to convince Athena.

But Athena wouldn't let up. "It really wouldn't matter if I knew them or not. What I'm saying is that the right woman could steal any man away. That woman may never enter Tom's life, but if she did, she could steal him away from Kate."

There was a silence in the room for a moment, and then Athena relentlessly continued, "The right person could steal anyone away, and that goes for the great Tom Verdi." Athena couldn't help but think to herself, *Give me an hour with that guy. I'd have him in the sack in two shakes.*

"Well, I guess that is an interesting perception with some truth to it." Yolanda didn't believe it for a second, but she wanted to drop the topic.

As both woman lost interest in the conversation, Athena put her head down and finished her work. She didn't know Tom Verdi or what kind of man he was. She had never even met the guy, but her perspective was that she knew *men* and what they were capable of. Most of all, Athena knew their weaknesses. She strongly believed that all men came from the same mold—at least, all the men in her life.

Athena had reached a conclusion about people in general. Most everyone would sell out at some point—for the right price, at the right moment. Given the right opportunity, anyone was capable of selling out for one life-altering experience. And this Tom Verdi was no exception.

Eleven

It was early evening, with the sun still shining through the lavishly dressed windows. The billowy, pale-yellow fabric above the windows enhanced the turquoise-plastered wall. An enormous mirror with a thick black rustic frame hung over the eggshell-colored, oversized sofa. The other rooms were painted in severe striking colors, in contrast to the wood floors. Everything that hung on the walls was strong, dark, and dramatic.

There was only one framed photograph in the boldly decorated town house. The picture was of a woman standing behind a little girl who was holding her rag doll. The woman had her arms wrapped around the little girl tightly, as if never to let go. The mother had tickled her daughter as the snapshot was taken, and the laughter lived on in their smiles.

The little girl had grown up to be the woman taking a shower down the hallway, and the day they took that picture was one she would never forget. Stepping out of the shower, she grabbed a towel and had begun to dry off when the phone rang. Soaking wet, she raced in urgency across the hall to answer the phone, leaving a trail of wet footprints behind her. When she picked up the receiver, no one responded on the other end of the line. It was the third time in several days that it had happened. Athena wasn't bothered by it, but she wondered if it could possibly have been her mother, with whom she hadn't spoken in four years.

Athena had tried to contact her mother, Margaret, twice after she left Chicago. A year after the wedding, she had called to let her mother know she was okay. Her mother, still devastated, had responded coldly to Athena and blamed her entirely for what had happened. The conversation had ended with Margaret sobbing and hanging up on her daughter. Six months later Athena had tried again, to no avail. Further attempts had ended with Athena hanging up before she finished dialing. Now four years later, Athena was beginning to wonder if she would ever see her mother again. She looked down at the picture briefly, then walked back into the bathroom to put on a tank top and sweatpants.

That night she lay on her fluffy white sofa, wrapped up in a blanket and wishing it was her mother's arms. There were two glasses of expensive wine on the coffee table, but only one glass was empty. The other was for the person in the picture that she held next to her heart as she fell asleep.

On Monday morning, Athena woke up feeling refreshed and ready to start the day. She got dressed in the new clothes she had purchased a few days earlier, and then walked out to her silver Corvette. She pressed the button to retract the black convertible top, exposing her to the Santa Barbara Highway. Driving along the coast was amazing. Athena had her right hand on the steering wheel as her left arm rested on the top of her door. The sun was shining on her gorgeous red hair, which drew attention from other drivers on the road.

When she arrived at the Bacara Hotel, Athena pulled into her designated parking space and hopped out of her car. She grabbed her new Chanel bag and strutted into the resort. Athena thought nothing of spending money she really didn't have. Anytime she bought something really expensive, she put it on a credit card and paid it off later. She loved expensive things and denied herself nothing.

Gliding through the lobby, she glanced over at the bellboys, none of whom greeted her as they usually did. She spotted Leon, the bell caption, talking to a customer.

"Hi, Leon," she said with a flirtatious smile. Leon just lifted his head in acknowledgment and continued talking to his customer. Leon had always gone out of his way to greet Athena, and on occasion he would even introduce her to his customer. She felt the distance and wondered if he was mad at her.

As she approached the door to her office, she saw Travis, the waiter from the restaurant, turn the corner. Travis had his head down, but he looked up as he noticed Athena. "Hey, honey," he said in a low voice.

"Hi, Travis. Are you okay?" she asked.

Travis said, "You haven't heard?"

"Haven't heard what? What's going on, Travis? Everyone is acting so weird. What is it?"

Just then, the door to Athena's office opened. She expected to see Yolanda inside, but instead her boss, Fred Yokulvitch, was standing at the door.

"Hi, Fred. I—"

"Athena," he interrupted her, "would you come inside here, please?"

"Sure," she said, unsure of what was about to take place. She looked over at Travis and realized something was terribly wrong. He shook his head from side to side and then walked away. A million things raced through Athena's mind. Had someone from her past contacted them? Had Fred found out about Jolie and the wedding? Had something happened to her mother?

Fred sat at Yolanda's desk and asked Athena to sit down as well. She was unnerved as Fred obviously searched for the right words. Finally he cleared his throat and said, "I have some bad news, Athena. Yolanda died yesterday."

"What?" she said, stunned. Her shoulders fell as she listened, finding it difficult to accept what Fred was telling her.

Fred held back his tears and continued, "She and Bert had just gotten back from church when she complained of feeling dizzy. She went into her bedroom to lie down a while. A little later, Bert went to check on her and she was gone."

Athena sat in disbelief. She hadn't known Yolanda all that well, but she appreciated the help and consideration Yolanda gave her during her trial period at her new job. At a time when she was missing her mother so, Athena had gravitated toward Yolanda. She remembered how Yolanda made her feel welcomed and took her to lunch when she did her first financial report. Athena didn't usually latch on to people, but she had felt comfortable around Yolanda.

Athena's eyes welled up with tears. As one fell to her cheek, she wiped it with her hand. Reaching over to get a tissue, she noticed the picture on Yolanda's desk and remembered their conversation about Tom Verdi. Athena felt bad about the things she had said, and she wondered why she hadn't just let the lady continue to believe that faithful love does exist. Maybe Yolanda had found that with Bert.

Fred put his hand on Athena's shoulder, exposing his age and a gold wedding band. "It's going to be a hard day," he said respectfully. Then walked over to the door and opened it, looking very tired and sad. "The funeral will be on Thursday," he said. He started to walk out, but then turned back and added, "If you need the rest of the day off, take it."

"No, no," Athena said. "Everyone is going to be sad, so I'll stay here where we all feel the same. Anyway, we can't all go home. We'd have to shut the place down." No other words were spoken, just the understanding that someone very special was gone. They gave each other the same sad smile, and then Fred walked out, leaving Athena to cry alone in the office.

The days that preceded the funeral were melancholy at best. Everybody was trying to contain their emotions as they reminisced about the late Yolanda Valdez. More than half the employees had to skip the funeral because they had to work. Athena was invited to attend, since she had worked in the same office as Yolanda and didn't need to work that day.

She pulled up to the chapel wearing a short black suit minus the blouse, her signature auburn ponytail, and dark sunglasses. Across the road sat the gray hearse that had delivered the woman to be remembered. Athena opened her car door to extend her shapely bare leg and proceeded to strut up to the mourners gathered in front of the small white church. She reached the top of the stairs and paused for a moment, surveying the group for anyone she knew.

"Only you could look this steamy-hot at a funeral," someone whispered in her ear.

Athena turned around to see Bob standing behind her, peering through his dark glasses. Relieved to see him, she said, "Oh God, I'm glad you're here. This is so depressing, and I've never been to a funeral."

"Really?" Bob asked. "I've been to a million of them. Everyone I know is dead."

"What?" Athena asked.

"Well, not everyone, but almost everyone." Glancing around, he continued, "I don't recognize any of these people. Do you? Not to mention that it's hotter than hell."

People were starting to line up to pay their respects. Bob and Athena moved up toward the line as they continued their conversation. Athena didn't realize that she was about to view the body. She had always managed to avoid funerals at church when she was a child. She would make up some excuse and Joliet would always cover for her.

They were approaching the open casket, when Athena peered through the crowd to see the bodacious floral arrangements displayed around the coffin. Suddenly, without warning, she was staring into the dead face of Yolanda. Never having seen the lifeless body of a human being before, Athena was paralyzed. The once meaningless conversations she had with Yolanda seemed to pop out in her memory.

Athena noticed how the woman's lips appeared rigidly tight. She glanced down at Yolanda's hands, which were crossed with one on top of the other. She had the same bronze nail polish that she had always worn. Athena noticed that her wedding ring had been removed, which she thought was odd because it was only a thin band.

"Why did they take her ring off?" she whispered to Bob. "That is so weird, because she loved that whole marriage thing. She'd be pissed off if she knew they took her wedding ring."

Athena and Bob followed other mourners up the aisle of the church, until they turned into a pew to sit down. The room began to fill with Yolanda's family, friends, and co-workers.

"This whole church gig gives me the creeps," Athena said. "I always feel like something fucked up is going to happen."

Just then, the golden brown casket glided past their pew, with the ten pallbearers directing it up to the altar. The priest came out and conducted the vigil and eulogy. Various family and friends were going up to tell stories and share their experiences with Yolanda.

Bob whispered to Athena, "I'm going up."

"What?" she said.

Before she could stop him, Bob stood up and walked to the front of the church. He told a cute, short story of when he and Yolanda had met years earlier. He was always trying to get her into a gym, he said, and she was always trying to get him into a church. At the end of his story, he made everyone chuckle by declaring that she had finally won.

Athena and Bob were whispering back and forth, when she glanced up at the podium and saw another man telling a story about Yolanda. As the man continued to speak, he attracted more of Athena's attention. She liked the way he was dressed and his striking dark hair. He had a thin goatee, and something about him was familiar. Athena sat still, listening to everything he had to say and scanning him from head to toe.

"Now that guy's my type," she whispered to Bob.

He looked up quickly to get a look at his competition. With relief in his voice, he said, "Tom? He's everyone's type. Shit, he's even my type."

Athena listened to Tom and then said again, "He's hot."

Bob agreed. "Every woman digs Tom, but he's married with two little kids." Athena remained quiet. Then Bob pointed up to the third pew and added, "See that little blond head up there in the third row? That's his wife."

Athena looked at the blond head and then back at the handsome man at the podium, as she listened closely to what he had to say. "He's attractive," she said quietly.

"Once again, he's *married*," Bob insisted. A minute later, he leaned into Athena and said, "Not only is he married—he's married, married." Athena didn't respond.

After everyone had finished their stories, the priest concluded with a blessing and a lovely prayer. Athena bent down to pick up her purse as the coffin rolled past her pew.

She looked up and tried to catch the eye of the pallbearer with the goatee, who had caught her attention at the podium. *Wait a minute,* she thought. *Tom?* She searched her memory for how she knew that name, and then she made the connection.

"Bob, is that the Tom who Yolanda was talking about?" Bob heard her, but he was being hurried out by the crowd behind him. Athena thought for a moment and then asked Bob, "What's his wife's name?"

"Kate," he answered.

"Kate," she said, confirming her memory. "That's the couple Yolanda was talking about," she said to herself.

Athena was no longer listening to Bob. She was trying to remember every detail that Yolanda told her about that couple. She remembered how the conversation almost got combative. Yolanda had praised Kate so much—her beauty and domesticity.

Athena reflected on how perfect her mother and their home had been, but still her father had left them. She blew it off as a ridiculous thought, that someone could be so naive as to think anyone was above infidelity. Athena held onto her beliefs. Yolanda had been a stupid, stupid woman, but she had also been a well-liked person who deserved respect, so Athena—in her mind—dropped the subject.

Outside the church, family and friends hugged each other, and everyone was invited to the Valdez home. Only Bert and his two sons were to be at the burial.

"Are you going to Yolanda's house?" Bob asked Athena. "There's going to be lunch there."

"No, I don't think so." Then Athena noticed her boss. "Look, Bill, there's Fred and his wife." Fred noticed Athena and Bill at the same time, and he walked over and hugged them both.

"Hi Fred," they said, greeting him and his wife.

"A sad day, isn't it?" Fred said.

"Yes, very sad," everyone agreed.

"You're both going to the Valdez home, aren't you?" Fred asked.

"I am," said Bill, "but Athena is going home."

Just then, Athena noticed Tom walking across the road to his car. He had his hand loosely on Kate's lower back, protectively escorting her across the street. "No," Athena said, "I'm going." She looked back at Tom and Kate, who were already in their car. "It'll help ease the pain," Athena added, but that was just words falling out of her mouth.

Fred said, "Fine, then we'll meet you both over there." He and his wife got in their car.

Bob said to Athena, "I didn't know you were such a brown nose."

"What do you mean?" she asked.

"Two minutes ago, you were leaving. But the boss walks over and suddenly you're all about 'It'll help ease the pain.'"

Athena went along with it. "Well, yeah, Bob. You know, job security," she said with a hint of flirtation.

"Well, I'm glad you're going. Hopefully we can get a couple of good cocktails out of it." They both laughed.

They followed the procession to the small but comfortable house. The aesthetics of the home were humble, but the garden held an abundance of bright purple bougainvilleas. The lawn was perfectly manicured and it was obvious the home was well cared for. Since it was a Santa Barbara residence, the value was astronomical.

People were beginning to pull up in front of the Valdez home, and soon there would be nowhere to park. Athena managed to squeeze her Corvette into a tight spot. A few cars behind, she saw Tom's car. She pulled down her visor and looked in the mirror to freshen her makeup. In the mirror, she tried to see the Verdis. She didn't really want to meet them, but she was curious about what they had that everyone seemed to admire.

Tom and Kate sat in their car for a moment, and then it was Kate who first got out. Her suit was different from Athena's, but her pale blond, shoulder-length hair was striking and she had an attractive way about her. Still, Athena didn't see what all the fuss was about.

She saw Bob's car pull up, and she wanted to go inside before he parked. She knew that it was always important to make an entrance, just in case there was someone inside who might be worth impressing.

Athena always kept a little bottle of oil in her glove compartment, so she took some out and rubbed it on her bare legs. She sprayed a splash of musk on her wrists and got out of her car. With her car door still open, she reached under her jacket and doubled up her waistband, making her skirt even shorter—a trick she had learned from Joliet. None of this was for Tom. She just enjoyed assuring herself that she was the most attractive woman in the world. After all, someone had to be.

Waiting for what she thought was the perfect moment, Athena walked up to the front door and entered the house. She looked around and saw no one she recognized. *Good*, she thought to herself. *Now I don't have to make needless conversation.* As she walked slowly into the living room, she could see the back of Kate's light blond hair through the crowd in the kitchen, and she knew that Tom would be close behind. When Athena noticed her own reflection in a huge mirror that hung in the hall, she stopped, stared at it, and then walked straight toward the kitchen.

Just as Athena was entering the kitchen, Tom took Kate's hand as they walked together into the backyard. Neither of them saw Athena.

Athena was greeted by various people, and then Bob walked in. "There you are," he said. She smiled and they both walked into the living room. For nearly two hours, they talked about Yolanda, ate various Cuban dishes, and drank wine. They never saw Tom or Kate.

The following morning, Kate and Tom were sitting in the Bacara Resort restaurant having brunch. They were staying at the resort for a couple of days. Their children were staying at Cynthia's home, allowing Kate and Tom some time alone.

"Did you get hold of Bert, honey?" Kate asked Tom, who was reading the morning paper.

"No, but I left him a message to call me if he needed anything." Then Tom continued in a more somber voice, "I still can't believe she's gone."

"I know," Kate said.

"I mean, I can't even picture Bert without her," Tom said. "I don't know what he's going to do."

The jingle of Kate's cell phone in her purse interrupted their conversation. She looked at the screen, said "Uh-oh," and answered the call.

"Hey, Katie," the caller said. The pleasant sound of Kate's best friend's voice was on the other end.

"Cynthia, how are the kids?" Kate asked. She could hear them crying in the background.

"Well, I don't know what the deal is, Katie." Exhaustion and frustration were apparent in Cynthia's voice. "They've both been crying since you left. They were okay for about thirty minutes, but then Tyler started crying and he hasn't stopped."

"Oh my God," Kate said in a disappointed voice.

"He cried all night," Cynthia said.

"Oh shit." Kate knew what was coming next.

"Katie, I don't know how you do it. I'm going to lose it."

"Let me talk to Natalie," Kate said.

Cynthia tried putting the kids on the phone, but they both just cried more. The conversation ended with the agreement that Cynthia would drive the kids up to the resort and drop them off. She was only an hour away.

"Well, what happened?" Tom asked.

Kate explained the children's behavior, but that didn't make it any easier for Tom. In an angry voice, he said, "You have got to be shitting me."

"I couldn't leave Cynthia stranded another night with them crying like that," Kate said. "I don't know what it is. Tyler has been like this for the past two months."

"And what's Natalie's excuse?" Tom asked, still angry.

"Well, she's not usually like that," Kate said in Natalie's defense. "She might be lonesome and tired of Tyler's crying."

"Yeah? Well, that makes two of us. I was really looking forward to being alone with you for once. Take a bath and sleep naked without them up our asses."

"I'll get them to fall asleep early," Kate said softly, "and we can still be together."

"That's just not what I had in mind," Tom said. "I don't want you using all your energy getting them to fall asleep—and still they end up in our bed. They're always in our bed. I mean, we can never get away from them."

"They're our kids, Tom. We're never going to get away from them."

"You know what I mean, Kate."

A few minutes later, while sipping his coffee, Tom looked up and saw a very pretty girl walking across the lobby. She wore a white fitted skirt with a white blouse and high-heeled sandals. It was refreshing, after all the black they had seen in the previous days. As the woman got closer, he noticed that she was more than just pretty—she was extremely beautiful. Her long red hair was pulled back in a ponytail, and he watched her until she was out of his sight.

"Hey," Tom whispered to Kate, "let's get upstairs before they come." Kate got her mood back and they got their check.

Later that afternoon, Athena was leaving the gym in her workout attire, sweaty and ready to go home for a shower. She stopped at her office to gather some data, and on her way out, she stopped at the restroom. Leaving the restroom and eager to get home, she flung the door open and quickly walked out, running into a little girl.

"Oh, little girl," Athena said, "I'm so sorry. Are you all right?" The little girl just stood there staring at her. Athena was about to continue on when she noticed that the girl was holding a cloth doll like the one Athena held in her picture. "What's this? May I see it?" She took the doll from the girl, studied it closely, and asked, "Where did you get this doll?"

The little girl answered shyly, "My mommy got it for me on cacation."

Athena asked, "Do you know where she got it?"

"No," the little girl said, "but I think Cacago."

Athena giggled and asked, "Do you mean Chicago?" She turned the doll over to check the back of the neck. She examined it to see if there was a tear, but there wasn't. "It could have been sewn up," she said out loud. Then she thought to herself, *Oh, that's ridiculous. It couldn't be the same doll.*

As she handed the doll back to the little girl, she looked into the child's eyes. Until that moment, she hadn't realized how much the little girl resembled herself as a child. She touched Natalie's hair and said, "You know, my hair used to be this color when I was little."

Just then a woman's voice interrupted her. "Natalie, don't ever disappear like that again."

Athena looked up into the face of the blond, perfect Kate. Something about Kate *was* special, she thought, as Kate took Natalie's hand.

Kate was in a hurry to get back to Cynthia, who was in the lobby dropping off the kids. She smiled at Athena and said, "I'm sorry."

Athena said, "Oh, don't be. Your little girl is adorable." She studied Kate, looking for some imperfection but not finding it.

Kate took Natalie's hand and they walked back into the lobby area, where Cynthia was sitting with Tyler.

Athena peeked around the corner looking for Tom, but he wasn't around. Then she grabbed her towel and went home without another thought of him.

The next day, Athena was working at her desk when she got a call from Fred. He told her that Bert was coming to the resort that afternoon to collect Yolanda's personal belongings. He asked Athena if she could gather Yolanda's things together, and she agreed.

Athena took everything out of Yolanda's desk and put it into a box. Then she did the same with the things on top of Yolanda's desk. When she picked up the picture that Yolanda had of herself and the gang at the housewarming, she started to put it into the box. But then she stopped, took another look at it, and thought to herself, *That guy is fucking hot.* She opened the back of the frame and took the picture out. She put it inside her purse and put the frame at the bottom of the box. If anyone asked, she would say she had no idea what had happened to the picture.

Several months later, Kate was in the kitchen cooking breakfast for Tom and the kids. "Honey, could you put Tyler in his high chair? His eggs are ready."

Tom picked up Tyler from the kitchen floor and put him in his chair.

Kate gave Tyler his breakfast and then went back to the stove for two more plates of food. "Natalie, come on, honey. Breakfast is ready." Natalie came running into the kitchen as Kate put down one plate for her and the other for Tom.

"Looks great, hon," Tom said as he picked up his fork.

Kate walked over and poured herself a cup of coffee. "Tom, could you pass me the cream, please?"

Tom reached for the cream. But before he could get it, Natalie grabbed it and swung it over to Kate, knocking the hot coffee into Tyler's lap. In an instant, the table turned into chaos.

Tyler's legs were red and painful, and he was crying hysterically. Kate quickly pulled him out of his high chair and tended to his wound.

Tom was clearly agitated with the situation, but he didn't blame Natalie.

"I'm sorry, Daddy," she said, starting to cry.

"It's not your fault, Natalie," Tom said. "But how many times have I asked you not to grab things when Mommy asks me to get them?"

Kate just looked at the two of them while she held ice on Tyler's knees.

Natalie walked into the living room and got Tyler's stuffed rabbit. "Look, Tyer. Look at Robbie," she said, trying to get his attention.

"Robbie," Tyler said. He took the stuffed rabbit and stopped crying.

"I'm sorry, Tyer," Natalie said. Kate put her arm around Natalie and gave her a kiss on her forehead.

"Is he okay? I've got to go to work," Tom said.

"Yeah, he'll be fine," Kate assured everyone.

Tom kissed Kate and the kids, and then he headed out the door. "I'll call you later," he told Kate.

Kate smiled and said, "Okay."

Later that afternoon, Tom was sitting in his office and going over his bills. He found an error on his credit card statement. The Bacara Resort had charged him two months in a row for the same weekend. He picked up the phone and dialed the resort, where the man at the front desk connected him to the accounting department.

The woman who answered the phone had an obviously young, flirtatious voice. "Hello, this is Athena Martine. May I help you?"

Instantly responding to the sound of her voice, Tom deepened his own voice slightly and said, in a sexier tone, "Yes, hello. I stayed at your resort a couple of months ago and was charged for that weekend. But now I see on my current statement that I've been charged again."

"Oh, multiple billings. That's a bummer," Athena said.

"Yeah," Tom said with a chuckle.

"Okay, let's take a look at that." She asked for his phone number and said, "It'll just take a moment for me to pull up your file. How was your stay with us? Did you use all of our amenities?"

Tom didn't want to get into the details of the funeral, so he just said, "Yes, it's a great place and we enjoyed it very much."

"Which massage did you get?" Athena didn't know who he was, but she always enjoyed flirting. She also knew the power in it. With a few seductive words from her, he would be hanging up a happy customer.

Tom told her that he had had the Swedish massage the last time he was at the resort.

"I love the deep tissue massage," Athena said, looking at her computer but not paying attention to it. "Deep tissue's the only way to go."

Tom didn't reply. His mind wandered to her comment. He didn't know whether this woman was toying with him, but he was enjoying it nonetheless.

"Okay," Athena said, with a hint of flirtation in her voice, "let me pull up your account."

It had been a long time since Tom had flirted with anyone on the phone. *The last person I flirted with was probably Kate,* he thought to himself.

"Can I have your name?" Athena asked.

"My last name is Verdi. Tom Verdi."

Athena pulled up his name before realizing who he was. It had been months since she'd heard his name, and it wasn't until she saw the name *Kate* that she got the connection.

"Your name is Tom Verdi?" Athena dabbled on her computer for a second and then asked, "May I put you on hold for a moment?"

"You're going to put me on hold?" Tom asked, slightly annoyed. "Should I call back? I'm kind of pressed for time."

"What do you think I'm going to do, go to lunch or something?" Athena asked. "I'll put you on my lap, and you can watch how fast I fix this error." They both chuckled.

I'm sorry," Tom said. "I don't mean to sound impatient. It's just that when hotels put you on hold, they take forever."

"I promise you, Tom, that I'll be right back."

Tom replied, "Okay, you promised." This was sure a more exciting conversation than most, he thought. It seemed like forever since he had experienced a fleeting moment with a stranger. He didn't know the person on the other end of the line and she didn't know him, so all the flirting in the world wasn't going to hurt anyone.

Tom thought back to the days in Canandaigua—how the girls had been obvious about their attraction for him. He loved his life now, but it had gotten stale. So the dangerous feeling he was getting from the conversation was amusing.

Athena had intentionally put Tom on hold. She didn't know the guy and had seen him only once, months ago. But now he was on the phone, and suddenly she was aroused by it. All the information she needed was already on her computer. She got back on the phone and asked, "Okay, you were here on the seventh, correct?"

"Yes," he answered.

"Okay, hang on." Then she changed the subject by asking, "Were you here with a girlfriend?" She already knew the answer, but she wanted to hear what he would say.

"No, I was there with my wife." Tom was reluctant to mention Kate only because he was enjoying the flirtation, but he also knew the game was over and it was time get back to reality.

"Oh, your wife. There's always a wife," Athena said with a giggle.

Athena didn't really appreciate her job at the resort. The minute something better came along, she would be gone in a heartbeat. But right now, she was thoroughly enjoying flirting with Tom. In a situation like that, she would take it all the way.

"I don't understand it," she said. "All these guys come to the resort with wives. Don't their wives give them massages?" She decided to continue to play the same card, thinking that she had nothing to lose. "When I get married, I'm going to give my husband a massage every single night."

"Really?" Tom asked. "Well, sometimes it's nice to get one from a professional."

"Well, I love giving massages." Then Athena added quickly, "I took masseuse and belly-dancing classes in college, so I'm kind of a professional."

"Really, you took those courses in college?"

"They were the two courses I really enjoyed," said Athena.

Tom's eyes widened and he felt himself getting excited by the conversation. Surprised, he asked, "Where did you go to school?"

"I went to Chicago State."

"Really? They teach belly-dancing classes in college?" he asked.

"Yeah. Well, I took extensive math courses and the belly-dancing course really helped me relax. I ended up excelling in both classes."

Tom was starting to think he should get off the phone. Suddenly he felt like he was at a strip club getting a lap dance. "I was a math major myself, so I know what you mean about the pressure."

"Oh, are you an accountant?" Athena asked, already knowing the answer from her conversation with Yolanda.

"Yes," Tom said.

"Well, here I am, going on about math courses when you're a math wiz yourself."

Tom said, "I don't know if I'd call myself a math wiz."

"Oh, *I* am," Athena said. "I've always loved math. I used to stun my teachers."

"Really?"

"Yep."

"Wow, we're looking for a math wiz," Tom mumbled to himself. Before the last word was out of his mouth, he realized his mistake.

"Really? What position do you have available?" Athena asked, trying not to sound overly interested.

"Oh, I was just kidding," Tom said, trying to backpedal.

"Okay, I get it. You don't like fat lesbians."

Tom exclaimed, "What?"

"While we've been talking, you went on our website and saw my picture. So now you want to avoid telling me about the position," Athena said, knowing there was no such website.

"No, no," Tom said. "I didn't even know you have a website."

"Well then," Athena said, "I'll tell you right off the bat that I'm a little overweight and I'm a lesbian. If you don't have a problem with that, you can call me and let me know if there's an opportunity available."

Tom was annoyed with himself for getting into this situation. Their conversation had gone in a completely different direction. What had begun as a simple flirtatious inquiry had turned into an interview appointment.

"You're in Thousand Oaks, correct?" Athena asked, changing her tone of voice completely. She knew that she had Tom hanging by a fragile thread, and she didn't want to lose the chance for that interview.

"Yes, we're in Thousand Oaks," he confirmed.

Ready to close the deal, Athena said, "You tell me what day and time you want me there."

Looking over his desk calendar, Tom saw an opening. "What about a week from tomorrow, the twelfth?"

"Perfect."

"One o'clock?"

"I'll be there. Thursday the twelfth at 1:00 p.m.," Athena confirmed. "Thank you, Mr. Verdi." Now she wanted to hang up.

"Hey, wait a minute," Tom said. "What about my account?"

"Oh, I had that fixed ten minutes ago."

"Oh, okay. Thank you," he said, unsure of what had just happened.

Athena hung up feeling like a champion. "What the fuck? I cannot believe what just happened," she said aloud. Then she threw her arms up in the air in triumph and yelled, "Yeah!"

Twelve

The following week was spent planning for the interview. Tom had been hoping that Athena would show up late so he would have an excuse not to hire her, but instead she arrived promptly at 12:50 p.m.

"Hello, I'm Athena Martine. I have an appointment with Mr. Verdi," she said to the receptionist sitting behind the front desk.

"Oh yes," Kelly said in her cheerful voice. "I'll let him know you're here." She picked up the phone and dialed Tom's office, informing him that Athena had arrived for her appointment.

A few minutes later, Tom came around the corner. The woman sitting on the sofa wasn't at all what he had expected. Her hair was parted in the middle and pulled back in a tight bun resting at the base of her neck. She was wearing thick-rimmed, nonprescription glasses and not a stitch of makeup. She wore a sweatshirt-style sweater, oversized and extremely frumpy, with a matching long skirt. Her flat ballet-type shoes were clean and comfortable.

Tom was absolutely relieved to see her. "Athena, hello. Thanks for driving in." As Athena stood up, Tom reached out to shake her hand. He liked her strong grip.

"Hi, Mr. Verdi. It's nice to meet you," she said.

"Call me Tom. Everyone here does. Why don't you follow me and we'll have our meeting back in my office." Tom now felt great about interviewing Athena.

Following Tom down the hall, Athena admired his strong upper body. He wore navy-blue dress pants and a beautiful raw-silk dress shirt. She liked the way he smelled.

"Do you have a résumé?" Tom asked.

"Yes, I do," Athena answered as she pulled it out of her briefcase-style purse. It was about that time that Tom realized Athena didn't have a weight problem. He looked her résumé over while asking questions. The interview lasted nearly fifty minutes. When it was over, Tom stood up and shook her hand once more.

"Well, Athena, it was nice meeting you. Let me look things over, and I'll give you a call next week."

"Next week?" she said, obviously disappointed. "I don't want to wait till next week. What's your objection to hiring me?"

Surprised, Tom was unsure what to say. "Objection? I just need to see where you would fit in."

"Well, I'm positive that I'd be an asset to your firm," Athena said. "Give me a chance, and I promise I won't disappoint you. I promise."

"Well, you're tenacious—that's for sure," Tom said, wavering about whether to give her the job. "You see, here's the other thing. I'm going on vacation in two weeks, and I don't know when I can get someone to train you."

"I'll be here on Monday," she said. "Train me, and then leave me here while you're away. That's why you hire people, so you can go on vacations and let your staff do the work."

Tom looked at the wall and then back at Athena. "Okay, you're hired. Be here on Monday."

Athena smiled and said in a calm voice, "I promise to impress you."

"Okay then, you'll have your chance."

The next day, Athena resigned from the resort and informed her landlord and friends that she was going back to Chicago. She told a sympathetic story about having to go back to be with her mother, and how sorry she was that she couldn't give more notice. Because her move was so quick, she didn't have time to get an apartment, so she put her stuff in storage and got a room at the Village Hyatt.

On Monday morning, she was at work twenty minutes early, dressed much like she had dressed for the interview. She was polite to everyone and very professional. By the end of the day, she had proved to be a fast learner who could quickly take on some of the job by herself. Everyone was impressed and, so far, liked Athena.

Kelly Stewart, the receptionist at the front desk, was an older lady with eight grandchildren and a warm voice. "How was your first day, dear?" she asked Athena.

"It was great, thank you," Athena said.

Typing on her computer, Kelly asked, "Is Tom showing you all the ropes?"

This time Athena answered in a distinctly different voice, "No, not *all* the ropes. Not yet."

Kelly took note of Athena's odd tone, but then just dismissed it and got back to her work.

Just then Tom walked up and said, "Kelly, you know Brian is coming back to work the day I leave, right?"

"Yes, I know. Everything will be fine," Kelly said, reassuring him.

"Where are you going?" Athena asked Tom.

"Canandaigua, in upstate New York."

"The chosen spot," she said, knowing it would draw a reaction.

"You've been to Canandaigua?" Tom asked, as if she'd been to the moon.

"No, but I'm from Chicago, and I've heard of Canandaigua and the Finger Lakes," Athena explained.

He shook his head in disbelief. "I didn't think I'd ever run into anyone who had heard of Canandaigua, especially here." Walking back to his office, he mumbled to himself, "What a small world."

Athena had never heard of Canandaigua before she worked at the Bacara Resort. Yolanda had mentioned it to her when she spoke of Tom and Kate. She told Athena that Canandaigua had been named by the Indians because of its pristine beauty. It was something Tom and Kate often mentioned when telling their friends about the special place where they had met.

The next two weeks were more of the same—training, trivial conversation, and Athena dressing in as matronly a way as possible. The one thing she was doing consistently was impressing them with her math skills.

On the day before the trip, Tom and Kate were at home packing. "Honey," Tom said adoringly to Kate, "did you pack my blue sweater?"

"Of course. That's the aphrodisiac sweater," she said, flashing her tongue at him. "That sweater makes me horny."

"The sweater does or I do? Take it out and I'll wear it tonight," Tom said. He grabbed her and they both giggled. Then he got serious for a moment and said, "I hope everyone at the office will be okay while I'm gone."

"Stop worrying, Tom. They'll be fine, and Brian will be there."

"Yeah well, I have that new girl who just started—although she did learn the accounting schedule quickly," he said, easing his own mind.

"See, if she does have a problem, she'll ask Brian." Kate hugged her husband and assured him that everything would be all right. They finished packing and then went to bed.

The flight to New York tested Tom's patience once again when Tyler threw his usual fit. "Is he ever going to get over this crying-on-the-plane thing?" Tom asked.

"It's his ears," Kate said, equally frustrated. "The doctor said that he will probably need tubes in his ears."

"Oh great," said Tom.

Kate confessed, "I didn't want to tell you before we left, honey, because I didn't want to worry you. I was hoping he would do better on this trip," she said, looking back at Tyler.

"Well, it doesn't matter now," Tom said. "Let's just get to Mom's."

Tom gathered the luggage and got a taxi into town. It wasn't until they arrived at his parents' home that he realized he had left his cell phone on the plane. He called the airport and had them FedEx it to where he was staying. The rest of the evening was spent visiting relatives, drinking in bars, and spending time with friends.

The following day, after spending the afternoon on the lake, Tom got his cell phone back from FedEx. When he opened the package, he saw that he had eleven missed messages. "Oh great," he said, "someone fucked with my phone." But then he noticed that they were all from Brian. "Oh shit," he said to himself. From where he was standing, he could see Kate and his family all sitting in the backyard and talking. Worried that something was wrong at the office, he dialed Brian's cell phone immediately.

Knowing it was Tom by the caller ID on his own cell phone, Brian greeted him in a serious tone. "Hi, Tom."

"Brian, what's wrong?" Tom asked.

"What's up with this chick you hired?" Brian asked. "What were you thinking?"

"Why? What's the matter? What's going on?" Tom asked, not knowing what Brian was referring to.

"What's going on?" Brian repeated in his deep voice. "Not a fucking thing since I got back to the office. Who wants to work with Miss Goddess Playmate sitting next door?"

"Who are you talking about?" Tom asked, confused. "Athena? What the hell are you talking about? You think she's hot?"

"Yeah," Brian said. "I've got a dick and I think she's hot."

Tom said in disbelief, "You've got to be kidding, man. Your taste in women sucks. You'd go for anybody."

"You've gotta be gay if you don't think she's the hottest fucking thing on this earth."

"Yeah, okay," Tom said facetiously. "Well, I'm on a trip and I really don't want to talk about your freak obsessions. Is this seriously why you called me eleven times? Oh, and by the way, she's a dyke."

"What?" Brian asked in a disappointed voice. "You gotta be shittin me."

"No, I'm not," Tom said. "She told me during the interview."

"Well, I'll tell you, bud, I'd like to watch that," Brian said, obviously fantasizing.

"Oh dude," Tom said, trying to convince Brian, "you must have been stoned when you saw her. She's not hot."

"Okaaaaay, married man who has obviously had his dick cut off by his wife. Did Kate meet her?"

"No, I don't think so. Why?"

"Because," Brian said, "I don't think Kate's gonna dig this situation."

"Kate won't be jealous of Athena, Brian."

"Dude, my mother would be jealous of her."

Tom just laughed.

"Laugh all you want, bro," Brian said. "I know chicks and they would *all* be jealous of her."

"Yeah, you know chicks all right," Tom said. "That's why you've been divorced twice."

"Well," Brian said, "I'm glad I'm divorced now."

"Unless you've got a vagina, it's not going to help you with this girl," Tom said, and they both laughed.

As Brian was sitting at his desk and talking to Tom, Athena walked in wearing a very short, flowing, floral chiffon dress. Her tan legs showed off her very high-heeled sandals. Her beautiful hair was pulled up in a shiny ponytail that accentuated her pink lips and dark, long-lashed eyes. This was a completely different Athena than the woman Tom had interviewed in his office.

She smiled and whispered to Brian that she had just finished the file he had given her. Then she walked out of his office, leaving behind the scent of fresh-cut flowers.

"Hey man," Brian said to Tom, "stay an extra week. Maybe I'll be remarried by the time you get back."

"Yeah, whatever," Tom said. "Just keep an eye on everything."

"Don't worry, I definitely will," Brian said, only half joking.

"You know what I mean," Tom said.

"Yeah, okay. Goodbye, Tom."

"Bye." Tom hung up, thinking to himself, *What a nut!*

Over the next couple of weeks, Tom caught up with family and spent time alone with his wife. They were enjoying the lake and eating out with friends while the children spent time with their grandparents. Tom would occasionally call the office, and he and Brian continued their little tit for tat.

They spent their last night in Canandaigua at Moonies with the funny Mike B., drinking shots of tequila and beer. Mike was his usual hilarious self, and Tom and Kate were enjoying every minute of it.

"Tom," Mike asked, "how did you get so lucky, to marry such an awesome babe?"

Kate snuggled into Mike's chest and said, "I love you, Mike."

"Will you just leave him and marry me? I'm better in bed," Mike said, sipping his beer. They all laughed.

"Let's do another shot," Tom said, flagging down the waitress.

"Tom, we're getting on a plane tomorrow," Kate said.

"Let's do another shot and live a little," Tom said, obviously drunk already.

The waitress brought over three shots, and Tom handed one to Kate and one to Mike. Lifting his own shot, he said, "Here's to the best wife in the world." Everyone gulped down their shots, and Kate gave Tom a deep kiss.

"Hey, hey," Mike said, "where's mine?" Kate leaned over and kissed him on the cheek.

A few minutes later the bartender yelled, "Last call."

Tom looked at his watch and said, "Shit, it's two o'clock. We'd better go, Kate." The three of them stumbled out of the bar and walked home.

The following morning, Tom woke up to the sun shining on his face through the window. "Oh no," he said softly, when he realized how bad he felt. He got out of bed and walked into the bathroom to find Kate throwing up.

"Oh my God," she said, slumped over the toilet bowl, "we can't get on a plane today. You've got to call the airport."

Tom replied in a slow, raspy voice, "I can't do that, Kate. I have to be back at the office."

"You're the one who ordered the shots," she said, giving him a dirty look. "Drink some more and live a little," she said, mocking him.

"I'll see if I can delay our flight till tonight," he said.

He postponed their flight until later that evening, which still wasn't enough time for Kate. She was sick for most of the trip home and almost unable to tend to Tyler. Tom did the best he could, but it was a miserable experience at best.

When they walked through the door of their home, they dropped their bags, ran upstairs, and all got into the same comfy bed. They were glad to be home.

Thirteen

Tom awoke surprisingly rested and ready to get back to the office. He got dressed, then walked over to the bed that Kate and the kids were sleeping in and leaned over to give her a kiss on her head. She didn't budge. He walked down the stairs and left her a note reminding her to pick up Moonies. He signed it, "I love you, baby," and then left for work.

Taking his usual route to his office building, Tom enjoyed the drive that morning. When he pulled into the parking lot, however, a decked-out silver Corvette was in his usual parking space. The license plate read "Goddess." "What the hell," he said, then realized that it must be "Athena, the Goddess of whatever" in his spot. *She's pissing me off already*, he thought to himself, parking his car by the trash bin. As he walked to his office, Tom checked out the Corvette and thought to himself, *You wouldn't think she would have a car like that.*

"Hey, Tom," Kelly said as he walked into the lobby, "welcome back."

"Thank you, Kelly," Tom replied. They exchanged some words about the previous weeks, and then Tom retreated into his office. No one was due at work until ten o'clock that morning.

Tom was sitting at his desk with his head down, entrenched in his reports, when he heard a knock on his open door. He looked up and saw a woman wearing a short white skirt and matching sleeveless jacket. Her long reddish hair framed her stunning looks, and she had gorgeous skin and a beautiful style. Suddenly he realized that it was Athena standing before him.

"Hi, Athena," he said slowly, confused about why she looked so different. He could now see what Brian had been talking about all week. "Excuse me for staring, but it's just that you look so different."

"I do?" she said, trying to sound surprised. "I didn't think anyone would even notice."

"What did you do different?" he asked as he tried to figure out what it was that had changed her looks so drastically.

"Oh well, this is sort of how I always dress," she said with a smile. She stretched out her long tanned leg, which looked perfect to Tom. "But I thought that everyone here, being accountants, might be really conservative, so I changed the way I dressed because I really wanted the job."

Tom was looking at her in shock. Never had he met anyone more intimidating. "So you just dressed that way to get the job?" he asked quietly.

"No," she said firmly. "I was going to change the way I look."

Tom just stared at her, thinking, *Why would anyone change the way they looked, if they looked like that?*

Then in a sweet voice she asked, "Is there a problem? Is it okay to dress like this for work?"

There was not much Tom could say. She looked extremely professional and took more pride in the way she dressed than anyone he had seen in the past. She was punctual and, based on the report Brian gave him, she got more work done in the time he was gone than half his crew put together.

Athena had only one fault, as far as Tom was concerned, which was that she was so beautiful that it might cause a problem among the staff. Not to mention that Tom himself felt a little uneasy being in the same room with her.

His breathing pattern changed when she entered the room, and he got a feeling in his stomach that he hadn't had since he first met Kate. He felt as if someone had gone into his brain and turned the lights on.

Suddenly he wanted to walk around the entire office and see what else had been going on since he'd been gone. In a few short minutes, his office had become unfamiliar to him. He could sense a stranger here. Why was he feeling this way all of a sudden? For a second, Tom thought it was ridiculous. *I need to go home and kiss my wife*, he thought, *and this will pass.* He had hired a dozen people before, all strangers, including a few very pretty girls, but he loved his wife. Tom adored Kate.

Athena interrupted his train of thought. "Tom, do you not like my outfit?"

As he glanced down her leg, only to find a high-heeled sandal showing off a very pretty red pedicure, he answered, "No, it's fine. You look very nice." *What's not to like*, he thought.

"Thank you," Athena said. Then she strutted out of Tom's office with a perky smile on her face and his eyes on her ass.

Tom looked at his watch with anticipation. *When the hell is Brian going to get here?* A few moments later, he heard Brian talking to Kelly in the front. He jumped out of his seat and walked over to where they were chatting.

"Hey, buddy," Brian said as he patted Tom on the shoulder. "Can I talk to you for a minute?"

"Sure," Tom said, and the two men walked back to Tom's office. As he closed the door, Tom looked at Brian for a moment without saying a word.

"What's going on?" Brian asked in a concerned voice.

"That's not the girl I hired," Tom whispered.

"Really? What do you mean?" Brian asked, confused. "You told me her name was Athena."

"No, that's the same girl, but she didn't look like that when she came in for the interview."

"That's what Kelly said, but I didn't know what the hell she was talking about."

"She looked totally different," explained Tom. "She had an old-lady bun on the back of her head and glasses."

"Yeah? Well, she had a ponytail all last week, and I still thought she looked hot," Brian said with a grin.

"No, you don't understand," Tom said.

But before Tom could finish, Brian interrupted him. "Who cares? She's doing a great job. She's hot, but let's just deal with it."

"Hey," Tom said, "wasn't it you calling me all last week, saying, 'Who can work with Miss Hot Pants Playmate working next door?'"

"Just give her a chance," Brian said.

"Oh yeah, now you're telling me to give her a chance. We've already spent two weeks talking about this woman. Not to mention that Kate's gonna shit when she finds out some hot chick's working in the office giving everyone boners."

"Ooooooh," Brian joked, "but I thought Kate wouldn't get jealous over something like *that*." Then he got more serious and said, "Give it about two weeks, Tom, and you'll be over the whole thing. And don't forget, she's a lesbian."

"Oh yeah, that helps?" Tom said. "That'll just fuel everyone's imaginations." They gave each other an eyebrow raise, and then Brian opened Tom's door.

Almost immediately, Athena walked in. "Hey, guys," she said in a friendly voice.

"You're doing a great job, Athena," Brian said, winking at Tom and walking out of the office.

Athena smiled and then handed Tom another file that she had finished before it was needed. She was flirting with him on a subtle level, which was tantalizing to both of them. She sensed his uneasiness and was enjoying the challenge.

Tom opened the file to find that it was thorough. Once again, Athena had gone beyond what was expected of her. He decided that he couldn't fire her. He would just have to get over the fact that he was instantly attracted to her. He was impressed by her strong work ethic, and he told her so.

She turned around, caught his eye, and said, "You're so welcome, Tom."

Athena walked back to her desk and sat down. *I want this guy,* she thought to herself. *This is going to be fun.*

Back at home, Kate awoke feeling tired. She was exhausted from the trip, and the kids had moved around in bed so much that she hadn't been able to get a good night's rest. Natalie and Tyler were still asleep, so Kate sneaked downstairs to get a cup of coffee. She walked into the kitchen and saw the note Tom had left on the granite countertop. She put the note into her robe pocket and walked over to the coffeepot, which Tom had turned on before he left. She poured a cup of coffee and walked over to the phone to call him.

"Hi, Kelly," she said. They chatted for a bit about the trip, and then Kelly transferred the call to Tom.

"Hey, honey," Tom said.

"Hi," Kate whispered.

"The kids up yet?"

"No," she said, "thank God. I can have a little peaceful time to myself. How are you feeling?"

"I'm fine," Tom said. "I got a good night's sleep."

"I don't know how, with the kids kicking every two minutes." Sounding half asleep, Kate said, "I feel like somebody's old grandmother." She was obviously unaware that a gorgeous woman stood only a few feet away from her husband, taunting him. Kate asked, "How was everything at work while you were gone? Was everything okay?"

"Oh, yeah, everything's great," he said, not ready to tell Kate that he had hired a goddess.

"How did that new girl do? Tina?" she asked.

"She's actually doing really well," he said. Nervous to say anything about Athena, he tried to change the subject. "Did you get my note?"

"Yes, and I love you too, baby," she said, sipping her coffee. "I'm gonna wait a little while before I pick him up."

Tom said, "Don't forget the dog food."

About that time, Athena walked by Tom's office, and he felt an urge to lower his voice. "I gotta go," he said, feeling slightly guilty. "Brian's waiting to talk to me."

"Okay," Kate said. "Call me later. Love you."

In an instant, Tom was so powerfully attracted to Athena, that it felt like being hit by a car. There was no warning. What Tom didn't know, and what Kate sipping coffee in her bathrobe didn't know, and what Natalie and Tyler asleep in their beds didn't know, was that their world was about to be turned upside down and changed forever. Their lives would never again be the same.

That day, Tom left the office early. He drove straight home, remembering every conversation he had shared with Athena. He pulled in his driveway, took a deep breath, got his briefcase, and went into the house. Kate wasn't in the kitchen, so Tom went upstairs, where he saw his two children playing together in Tyler's room. He quietly sneaked around them to find his wife. When he walked into their bedroom, he saw Kate combing her pale blond hair in the bathroom. Locking the bedroom door, Tom pulled his shirt off and anxiously walked toward Kate.

"Oh hi, honey," she said, continuing to comb her hair.

Tom walked up behind her without saying a word and put his hands on her breasts while kissing the back of her neck. Then he turned her around and held her face in his hands as he began to kiss her mouth. His tongue was engorged in her mouth as the brush fell from her hand to the floor.

When Tom grabbed Kate between her legs, she was instantly turned on. He motioned her to get on top of the bed. He unbuttoned her pants, pulled them down, and pulled her body strong against his face. He took one of her thighs and put it on top of his shoulder and began to kiss her aggressively between her legs, until she gasped for air as she climaxed all over his face. The sex was passionate and not like anything they had done in a long time.

The rest of the week was a trial period for everyone at work. Tom was searching for any reason to let Athena go, but she was always the first to arrive and the last to leave. She was aggressive and diligent, and Tom was trying to ignore the fact that although she dressed professionally, he also found it provocative.

He was aware that anyone should be grateful to have such a dedicated employee. Athena was a powerhouse, and he knew she would be an asset to his or any other company. But he also knew he had to get rid of her—and fast, because she was constantly present in his thoughts.

It was Friday evening at the office, and Tom was packing up his briefcase to leave. Brian walked by and said, "First week back is always a killer," acknowledging the tired look on Tom's face.

"Yeah, I'm gonna go home," Tom said. He told everyone good night and walked out to the parking lot. He got in his car and dialed home on his Bluetooth.

When Kate answered the phone, Tom said, "Hey, babe, I'm on my way home."

"Great!" she replied.

"What are you making for dinner?" he asked.

"Garlic and parmesan chicken."

"That sounds so good. I'm starv—" Tom's thoughts were interrupted by the sight of Athena leaving the office. He thought she had already gone, but she must have been working on something in the back office.

"Tom, are you there?" Kate asked.

"Yeah," he said as he watched Athena standing outside her Corvette. She stood beside her car combing her hair, and then she reached in behind her seat and pulled something out. Looking around to make sure no one was watching, she pulled her sweater off, exposing ample cleavage in a lacy black bra. Then she pulled the tank top over her head and hopped into her 'Vette. Grabbing her sunglasses from the visor, Athena drove off slowly. Before exiting the parking lot, however, she looked in her rearview mirror and grinned. "Bye, Tom. Have a nice weekend," she said, knowing all along that he was watching.

Later that evening, Tom barely touched his dinner. Kate commented on how he had said earlier that he was hungry, but then he hardly touched his food. Tom just brushed it off as being tired, and then he went and sat in the den. Kate tried several times to start a conversation with him, but he just sat there staring into space and hardly answering her.

"Tom, what's the matter?" Kate asked. "You don't seem like yourself, and you're not even listening to me."

"Oh, what did you say?" he asked with vague interest.

"You're not listening to me. What's the matter?" Kate repeated gently.

"Oh, nothing. I'm sorry, Kate. I'm just tired, and I think I'll go to bed."

"Go ahead. You need some rest," she said sweetly. "You went straight from the trip to working so hard. You needed a rest after that vacation." She kissed him good night and said, "Go ahead. I'll be up in a little bit."

Tom went upstairs, hoping he could shake it off, like a flu or something that could be cured with time. He lay in his bed thinking about Athena. He could still smell her fragrance. He thought about the intense way she looked into his eyes when she handed him the report and the way she had tossed her hair in the parking lot. He remembered how he had sat in his car watching her, like a voyeur, when she pulled her top off, thinking no one was looking. He had an excited feeling in his stomach thinking about her, and he couldn't get her out of his mind. He lay there for hours before he finally fell asleep, and then he tossed and turned all night.

The weekend was uneventful. Tom spent most of his time looking at his watch. He was irritable and nervous, but mostly he was bored. Nothing Kate or the kids said interested him. He was counting down the minutes until he would return to work on Monday.

Fourteen

I n the following weeks, Athena excelled tremendously. She demonstrated an impeccable work ethic, helping the other employees get their work done after she completed her own. She became familiar in the office and everyone liked her. The women were not threatened by her, especially because word got out quickly that she was a lesbian. Only Vivian, in the back, showed added interest in her. Tom maintained his innocence, despite his growing attraction for the new girl in the office.

Brian shared several lunches with Athena, reporting back to Tom on how funny she was. They also enjoyed many "happy hours" together, always inviting Tom to go with them. But he always insisted that he had to get home to his wife and kids.

One Friday afternoon, half the staff had left early for the holiday. Only a scattered few remained, including Brian and Tom, who were standing in the kitchen laughing. Athena took the opportunity to join in. She caught up on a couple of jokes and threw a few in herself, and they all laughed. Brian and Tom were surprised by her quick humor.

"What are you guys doing this weekend?" Athena asked coyly.

Brian was going fishing with both his brothers on Saturday.

"What about you, Tom?" she asked, looking at him with her dark-brown eyes.

"I'm not doing much," he said, unable to stop himself from looking at her. When she smiled, he could see slightly inside her moist lips, and her teeth seemed extremely white. He could smell a hint of mint when she spoke.

Athena tilted her head to one side and asked, "Why not?"

Tom had already forgotten the question. "Why not *what*?"

"Why aren't you doing anything?"

Tom knew he should lie, but he felt his body take control and answer for him. "My wife's going to San Francisco with her best friend," he said, knowing he had just made a grave mistake.

"You're kidding. Really?" Athena couldn't believe she was hearing this. "When is she leaving?"

"They actually left this morning," Tom replied.

Stupid woman, Athena thought. *Stupid, stupid woman.*

Brian was watching the conversation as if it were a tennis match.

Mustering all her charm, Athena wasn't about to pull any punches. "I've got a great idea," she said, flaunting her body subtly.

"Really? What?" Brian asked. Tom was equally interested.

"Let's go to a strip club," she said.

"What?" Tom asked, obviously surprised. There weren't any strip clubs in Canandaigua. Brian just laughed. Neither of them could believe their ears.

"I'm serious. I've been out here seven weeks, and all I've done is work." Athena put her hand on Brian's back and added, "I haven't had any fun. You know I've been working my ass off for you guys."

"Yeah, you have," Tom said. "You've been doing a great job, you really have." Brian agreed.

"Then let's go. Why not?" she insisted.

"We can't go to a strip club with an employee," Tom said firmly.

"Why not? It's not like I'm gonna pick you up." Athena grinned and stared right into his eyes, playing the lesbian card.

"It's not that," Tom said. "We can't go to a strip club with *any* employee. That's just a lawsuit waiting to happen."

Brian looked at Tom, then back at Athena. "Tom can't go, but I can," he said, acting less responsibly and ready to take advantage of the opportunity.

"No, you can't," Tom insisted.

"Great. All we need is one more," said Athena, sensing that she was making progress in talking Tom into it.

Tom really, really, really wanted to go, but he felt guilty because he was drawn to her—and the attraction he had for her was growing.

"Let's go," Athena whined, desperate to convince him. "No one will know, and it'll be a blast."

"You sound persuasive, believe me," Tom said.

"Then let's go," she demanded. "None of us will ever say a word. I've been working my ass off, and I want to have some fun. I want to go to a strip club. I don't know anybody else out here—just you guys."

Tom looked at Brian, who was obviously okay with it. Tom himself felt a need to have some fun, not to mention that he really was interested in seeing what Athena was like outside the office. He was praying that he would see something that would turn him off. "I know I'm gonna get my ass kicked for this," he said.

"No, you're not. Both of you meet back here at nine o'clock, okay?" Athena said, taking charge as if it were already decided that they would go.

Brian looked at Tom, and they both nodded.

"Okay then," she said, "it's a date."

"Don't say that. My wife will kill me," Tom said, worried about the potential consequences of the upcoming evening.

"Oh, right," Athena said, with a half smirk on her face. "You're going to a strip club with a lesbian and another guy. Which one of us do you think you have a better shot with?"

They all three laughed as they walked out of the office and confirmed their meeting time.

It was eight fifty-five, and just like always, Athena was punctual. The brown-eyed vixen drove up just in time to stop Tom from changing his mind. He had been wavering all evening about going to the strip club, but once again Athena and Brian talked him into it. The only thing that made Tom comfortable with going was the fact that Athena was gay.

Brian and Tom were standing beside Tom's car when Athena drove up. "What harm could possibly come from it?" Brian kept asking in a whisper. "She's a dyke. *We* think she's a fuckin' hottie, but don't forget, buddy, that the only thing she'd find interesting about you is your wife."

Tom hesitantly nodded as Bryan walked fiercely to the hot lesbian's car. "Athena, baby," he said in his suave, seventies way.

When she got out of her car, Tom couldn't believe his eyes. She looked sexier than anything he had ever seen. She wore belly-revealing, tight black pants and high-heeled sandals. Her jewel-pierced navel and amazing stomach looked fabulous. Her long, golden-red hair glowed against her short, black bra top. With those glossy lips, Athena was an absolute turn-on.

Athena was equally impressed with Tom. He stood tall, and his broad shoulders and strong arms were evident through his long-sleeve, button-down shirt. He wore it outside his jeans with barefoot slip-on shoes. His masculine features, combined with his dark hair and eyes, were scratchingly sexy.

"Hey, boys, are you ready for some fun?" she asked with a big grin.

Brian just blurted it out. "Holy shit, you look incredible!"

Tom was stunned into silence. Athena was even more beautiful than he remembered. She looked great at the office in her professional attire, and now she was taking it to a whole new level.

The men barely heard a word she said. They just nodded and got into Tom's car.

What have I gotten myself into? Tom thought to himself as he closed his car door. He knew without a doubt that he was in a ridiculously stupid situation. All he had to do was ask them to get out of his car, go straight home, and lock the doors—but he didn't. Something inside him just made him go along with it, like the apple and the snake.

Tom knew it was wrong to be where he was—in a car with a beautiful woman to whom he was attracted. He thought about Kate and how much he loved her. Nothing could ever come between them or change that, but an excited feeling was taking over his body. This was harmless. No one knew what he was feeling, and no one would *ever* know. This was a secret that he would take to his grave. The intense urge to stay where he was, combined with the fact that Kate was out of town, persuaded him to go ahead with the evening.

Even though Tom knew that Athena desired women, he found her more interesting and sexually alluring than anyone he had ever met. She was explosively charismatic and quick humored, always making them laugh, which was turn-on in itself. He was very impressed, as she had said he would be, but not in the way he was hoping. This was different from the way he felt about Kate. From the moment he met Kate, he had known she was the one. Kate was gorgeous and electrifying, and nothing could compare with the breathtaking sex they shared together.

Wrestling with his desires, Tom blurted out shyly, "You know what? I can't go." He was feeling tremendous guilt for even contemplating going, but before he could finish, Athena interrupted him.

"Will you shut up?" she said in her sultry voice. "I found out about this great club in LA. The girls have really big tits and they're all real—no boob jobs. It's supposed to be amazing." She was looking directly at Brian.

Brian leaned into Athena and said, "I can tell we're gonna be really good friends."

Then Athena pulled herself closer to Tom, sitting in the driver's seat in front of her, and whispered, "All we're going to do is have a really fun time. We're not going to do anything bad. Then it'll be back to work as usual."

Tom looked in his rearview mirror at Athena's reflection and asked, "What's it called?"

"The Octopus," she said, with a hiss.

They locked eyes for a moment in the mirror, and Tom found it impossible to turn away. Athena was in his car, they were heading for a strip club, and Kate was nowhere to be found.

"If I go in there, no one says a word to anyone," Tom insisted. "If Kate ever found out, she'd blow a gasket. Deal?"

"Deal," Brian said. "Trust me, dude. I know she'd be pissed."

Sounding annoyed, Athena asked, "She'd really get that mad?"

"Just a little," Tom answered facetiously.

"Why?" Athena asked.

"I don't know," Tom said. "Why do women get mad at those things?"

"Because they're insecure about their men," Athena said confidently. "I think it's ridiculous. The women I date never get jealous."

Tom's mind drifted off to the idea of Athena with another woman.

She interrupted his delicious thought by asking, "Have you ever cheated on your wife, Tom?"

"Never!" he said with conviction. "I would never, ever cheat on Kate."

Athena responded, "Never? Never say never."

"No," Tom insisted, "you don't understand. I love Kate so much. I would never cheat on her." Tom sounded almost like he was trying to convince himself. He had always felt that way, and until recently he had never doubted his own fidelity. But he was absolutely certain at that moment that he would never cheat on Kate.

During the ride to the strip club, Brian, Tom, and Athena talked about their lives and what had led them to their current lifestyles. Athena creatively sensationalized her story, using her eyes and tone of voice to enhance her spotlight. Tom found her immensely interesting.

When they arrived at their destination, Tom gave the valet his key while Athena and Brian ran up the entrance. A beautiful Asian woman with well-endowed breasts stood behind the desk taking fifty dollars from each person who entered.

"Fifty bucks?" Tom whispered to Brian. "You gotta be shittin' me!" It had been years since Tom had been in a place like that.

Brian paid her gladly, with his eyes glued to her naked breasts.

Athena led them inside as if she worked there. They sat down in a booth made of soft black suede. "Is this real?" Tom asked as he ran his hand across the back of the booth. He was embarrassed, realizing he had made the wrong decision by being there.

"I can't believe you, dude," Brian said. "You're at a strip club and you're checking out the fuckin' booth." Tom and Brian were unaware that Athena was ordering Grey Goose shots from the scantly dressed waitress.

The three shared a short, meaningless conversation until the waitress returned with six shots of Vodka. "Here ya go," the young blond said, as she placed two shots in front of each of them. Before anyone said a word, Athena lifted a shot glass and suggested that Tom and Brian do the same. Staring into her drink, she said, "You're going in the hole." Then she downed the shot and, without taking a breath, downed her second shot as well.

Brian choked as he fantasized about what Athena meant by her toast, which he hadn't heard before but really liked. Tom hesitated to drink his second shot so quickly, but his ego helped him chuck it down.

The room was dark and hazy as Tom surveyed his surroundings. The bright light in front of him was focused up toward three gorgeous women, dancing provocatively on a small round platform in the middle of the room. They were weaving in and around one another, all three blindfolded as they touched one another's enormous breasts. One girl was barefoot, and the other two wore calf-high, lace-up boots. As Tom sat there enjoying their performance, he more easily justified the fifty-dollar entrance fee. He appreciated the sophisticated clientele, who were mostly dressed in suits. They weren't just gawking, like he had seen among the common lowlifes associated with most strip club establishments.

The waitress returned, looking for another drink order. Athena ordered a Grey Goose martini and two beers. She looked at the two men and asked, "What kind of beer do you guys want?"

"How'd you know we wanted beer?" Tom asked.

"You don't want a beer?" Athena asked, sounding confused.

Brian placed his order and asked, "Tom? Sam Adams?"

"Yeah," said Tom, who was still interested in Athena's answer about the beer.

She placed her jeweled hand on top of Tom's and said, "It's guaranteed. All men love the three B's—beer, boobs, and blow jobs." Then she looked at Brian and added, "All straight men, that is."

Tom laughed, but Brian felt a need to defend himself.

"Relax, Brian," Athena said. "I'm just joking." They were all feeling the results of the two shots.

Tom was caught off guard by her masculine comments. He loved her pornographic frankness and felt himself becoming more intrigued with every word she spoke. He had absolutely never met anyone like Athena, but he could never see himself with a woman like her, even if she was straight and he was single. Her sexy, girlish magnetism pulled him in like a tornado, but he kept reminding himself that she loved only women—and that he was in love with his wife.

As the night progressed, Tom and Athena managed to hold their liquor, but Brian became obviously intoxicated. Leaving the club, they walked on both sides of him like bookends, helping him to the car.

Athena took the keys from Tom. "Let me drive," she said. "The last thing you need is a DUI." Without saying a word, he agreed.

As she drove back to the office, they recapped the night's events. Athena had both men laughing hysterically as she imitated Tom's reaction to the lap dancer at their table.

When they pulled into the parking lot at the office, Athena asked if Tom and Brian would be able to drive home.

"I'm fine," Tom said. "My buzz is starting to wear off, but I'll definitely drive this guy home."

"Hey, I'm fine," Brian said.

"Yeah, right. Get in," said Tom as he shoved Brian into the passenger seat of his car. Then Tom walked around to the driver's side and fiddled with his keys, trying not to look at Athena. Finally he said to her, "Thanks for insisting that I get out. It was quite an adventure."

"You don't have to thank me," she said. "I enjoyed it more than you did."

"Yeah," he said, in a breathy voice, "I bet you did." They both laughed.

As the two cars drove off in separate directions, Tom looked over at Brian, who was almost asleep, and said, "Good thing she's gay, buddy."

Fifteen

Tom and Kate were lounging in bed, comfortably naked and sexually satisfied. Tom had his arm around Kate and was looking at the ceiling. He had a feeling of contentment, something he hadn't felt in a long time. He had so much love for Kate, and he was realizing that he had lost touch with the importance of his family in recent months. Then his thoughts were interrupted by the voices of Natalie and Tyler outside their bedroom door.

Quickly, Kate put on her soft robe and said, "Come in, sweetie pies." The two adorable children came running in, climbed onto the bed, and got under the covers. Giggling and laughing, the happy family lay in bed and watched cartoons.

That morning, Tom was grateful to be with his family. As Kate was at the stove cooking scrambled eggs and pancakes, Tom snuggled up behind her. He glanced over at the kids, who were busy in the corner playing with Moonies. Coyly sneaking his hand up Kate's robe, he felt her bare ass. She quickly moved away and told Tom to stop as she looked over at the children to make sure they hadn't noticed.

Kate and Tom both giggled. "Sorry," he said, "but I can't help it. I love you."

She gave him a sweet smile and said, "I love you, too."

Then Natalie and Tyler joined in, "We love you too, Daddy!"

Tom hugged Kate from behind and whispered in her ear, "Let's have another baby."

"What?" Kate exclaimed.

"Let's have another kid," Tom said again.

From the look on Kate's face, it was obvious that she didn't agree. "Are you out of your mind?"

"No," he answered. "I'm serious. I really think it would be good for us."

"Good for *you* maybe. You work all day and I'm left without a life," Kate said as she grinned at him adoringly. "I've always got Jan working in the store for me. I don't get to work at the store as much as I'd like to, Tom, and I really miss it."

Tom was looking for anything that would glue his family together more tightly, anything that would keep his mind off Athena. "But the kids are getting easier. If we want another baby, now would be a good time."

"Good for *you* maybe." Kate put bread in the toaster and made herself too busy to talk further.

They finished their breakfast and continued to jokingly argue about having another child. When Natalie and Tyler realized what they were talking about, they quickly joined in. They were adamantly on Tom's side.

"See what you started?" Kate said as she cleaned off the table and ignored the rest of the comments on the subject.

Tom's next few weeks at work were productive. The phones were ringing off the hook, and everyone was writing new deals.

Athena seemed to be excelling faster than anyone. She had just signed up another client and was getting ready to leave for lunch when the phone rang. "Hello. Verdi and Associates. This is Athena."

"Hi," said a friendly female voice, "this is Kate Verdi."

Athena stumbled over her thoughts for a moment, but then said, "Oh wow, it's nice to meet you—over the phone anyway."

"Nice to meet you, too," Kate said. "Tom has said so many nice things about you, Athena."

"Really?" Athena was very aware that Tom was impressed with her work ethic, but she had wondered if he voiced his opinion to his wife.

Kate said, "Well, maybe I'll meet you later. I'm going to have lunch with Tom today, so I'll pop in and say hello."

"Oh, that would be great," Athena said, immediately deciding to take the rest of the afternoon off.

As Athena transferred the call to Tom, she felt a territorial resentment toward Kate. She kept an eye on the red flashing light that indicated that Tom had not picked up the line yet, and then the red light went still. She continued to watch the red light until it went dark, letting her know they had finished their conversation. Then she stared at it for a moment with a vindictive glare, grabbed her purse, and headed for the door without saying a word.

She got into her car and pulled out of the parking lot, then drove without a destination but with an overwhelming feeling of empowerment. When she realized where she needed to go, she sped up through a red light and then turned into a shopping center without ever braking. Pulling into the first space available, Athena turned her car's engine off and said out loud, "I am going to break them fucking up if it's the last thing I do." Then she grabbed her purse and headed for a lingerie store.

"Hello," said the saleswoman working on display.

Athena interrupted her and said, "I need a shelf bra, something that will make my tits look fantastic."

"What size are you?" the woman asked, walking straight to the bra section and sensing Athena's urgency.

"Thirty-six B and flesh color."

The woman thumbed through the bras until she found the right size and then handed it to Athena, directing her to the dressing room. Athena went into the small, ornately decorated room and, without closing the thick velvet drape for privacy, removed her blouse and bra, exposing her breasts. The saleswoman stayed close by but tried not to stare.

Then Athena asked her opinion. "This looks fantastic on me, don't you think?"

The saleswoman was forced to look at Athena, the shelf bra wrapping underneath her breasts and pushing her rose-colored nipples straight forward. She could not help but admire Athena's beautiful bosom, saying, "You look amazing, you do."

"This bra might do the trick," Athena decided.

Trying not to be intrusive, the saleswoman asked, "Is there a certain somebody you're trying to impress?"

Athena handed the woman the bra and said, "Yes, there is a certain someone, and I'm going to get him to leave his wife."

After that, the woman kept quiet as Athena finished getting dressed, paid for the bra, and left.

Later that day, Athena purchased the counterpart to the undergarment, a white, long-sleeve, silk blouse that buttoned in the back. It was absolutely the look that would drop any man to his knees. She would wait for the perfect moment to wear that outfit just for Tom.

Sixteen

Weeks had passed since Tom suggested to Kate that they have another child. He was at his desk, which had a window into the staff office so that he could keep a clear watch on his employees. In return, they had a clear view of him as well.

Athena was walking toward the employee lounge when she noticed Tom obviously having a confrontation with someone on the phone. Brian was already in the lounge eating a sandwich. As Athena walked in the lounge, she asked Brian, "Who's Tom arguing with?"

Brian said, "I don't know. Is he fighting with someone?"

"Looks like it," Athena said.

Chewing his sandwich, Brian said, "It might be Kate. I transferred her over to him a few minutes ago."

"Really?" Athena was barely able to contain her enthusiasm.

A minute later, Tom walked in the lounge looking for bottled water.

"Everything all right, buddy?" Brian asked.

"Yeah," Tom mumbled, "whatever."

Athena was determined to find out if he had been arguing with Kate. "Relationships suck sometimes, don't they?" she said, trying to get some indication of what they could have been fighting about.

Tom looked over at Athena and then back in the refrigerator, deciding not to say another word about it.

Athena, on the other hand, wouldn't let up. "So what's the deal? Is she spending too much money?"

"No, she's not spending too much money," Tom said, defending Kate. "It's nothing like that. She's not doing anything." Then it just slipped out. "No, it's just that … I thought it would be nice to have another kid, and she's not into it."

"*What?*" Athena blurted out, annoyed at hearing the antithesis of what she had anticipated.

Brian looked up and said, "Wow, buddy. I didn't know you wanted another kid, but that's great."

Athena, still digesting what she had heard, kept quiet. Finally she muttered, "I can't believe she doesn't want to have your baby."

"What? No, she wants my baby. I mean, just not right now." Tom was confusing himself, wondering exactly what it was that Kate *didn't* want. "We have two kids now, and I guess she has her hands full already. Well, I don't know … The kids are getting bigger and more self-reliant, and it would be nice to have a little baby in the house again."

Athena said, "Maybe she's bored. I mean, you can't blame her. She's got nothing going on all day but baby talk and bullshit, so she's got to be bored out of her mind." Athena knew that she was pushing the envelope with her condescending tone, but still she continued, "Who wouldn't be? I mean, honestly, Tom, wouldn't you be bored if you had nothing going on all day except baby talk?"

Surprised at her callous comment, Tom and Brian both looked at Athena, who sensed their cold stares.

Feeling a sudden need to defend his wife again, Tom said, "Kate has a lot going on. She does, and she loves staying home with the kids."

Athena said, "She might tell you that, Tom. And yet she doesn't want to have another baby, does she?"

Tom sat quiet for a moment, knowing there was some truth to what Athena was saying. She was putting thoughts into his head that hadn't been there before. Wasn't his wife happy? He had certainly thought so before this conversation.

"I'm sorry, Tom," Athena said. "I didn't mean to insult you or her." She was careful not to use Kate's name or refer to her as his wife. She was now calculating every word in the conversation. She knew that if she wanted to destroy Tom and Kate's marriage, she would have to implement her plan immediately. *Game on,* Athena thought to herself. *This is going to be fun.*

That night, on Tom's drive home from work, he thought about the conversation in the employee lounge. He wondered if Kate was bored with her life. It had never even crossed his mind that she might be unhappy. He thought about Kate and the kids, and about his mom and dad in New York. His mom had always seemed happy. He thought about his childhood, how he had always felt so safe and warm, and how the possibility of his mother being unhappy had never occurred to him. She had to be the happiest person on earth, because she was needed and loved so much. So why didn't Kate feel the same way?

Tom was about to call his mom when he became aware of a red flashing light in his rearview mirror. "Oh shit!" he said out loud. It appeared to be a police officer pulling him over. He pulled over to the side of the road and stopped the car, and a robust man in uniform approached his window. Ten minutes later, Tom drove away with a seventy-five-dollar speeding ticket. He was steaming mad, and by the time he reached home, he had a severe headache.

Walking into his warm, friendly home, Tom could immediately smell a delicious meal cooking in the kitchen. Kate and the kids were talking and laughing, and Moonies lay with his head resting on his paws in the middle of it all.

Still, Tom was mad. Mad at the cop. Mad about the ticket. Mad at Athena for suggesting that Kate was bored with her life. Mad at Kate for being bored with her life. But most of all, Tom was mad at himself for being bored with his own life.

He walked in the kitchen and was greeted with a paper airplane crashing into his face.

"Daddy!" Tyler yelled excitedly. He jumped on Tom, accidentally smudging a purple line down the front of Tom's silk shirt.

Tom looked down at his shirt, and then at the marker Tyler was holding. Furious, he exclaimed, "What the fuck?"

"Tom," Kate yelled, "it's only a waterproof marker. It'll come out." She grabbed a saddened Tyler.

Tom stared at his shirt. "I'm sorry, but what was he doing with it anyway?"

"He was coloring his paper airplane," Kate said as she held Tyler. "What difference does it make, Tom? Why are you acting like this? He's just a little boy. What's wrong with you?"

Tom said, "I'm sorry."

Tyler buried his head in his mother's lap.

Tom didn't say much else. He walked over to the cupboard, got two Tylenol PMs, and mumbled, "I'm gonna go upstairs. I'm just really tired."

Kate asked, "What about dinner? I made meat loaf."

"I'm not hungry," Tom said. "I had a big lunch."

Kate looked over at the stove, where she had a fantastic meal cooking, and felt disappointed.

Tom walked upstairs, took the sleep aid, and didn't wake up until the next morning. When he finally got up, he was starving, not having eaten dinner the night before. He looked around and didn't see Kate. He pulled on his navy-blue sweatpants, which were lying across the foot of the bed, and walked down the hall to find his children still asleep.

He went downstairs and smelled coffee brewing in the kitchen. Around the corner he saw Kate sitting at the breakfast nook and filling out a form. "What are you doing?" he asked.

"Oh," she gasped, grabbing her chest. "You scared me, honey." She caught her breath and said, "I'm filling out this volunteer slip to go on Natalie's field trip at school." Then she looked up at Tom and said, "Good morning."

"Good morning," he said.

She kept looking at him with a slight smile, waiting for an explanation for his behavior the prior evening. "Why were you in such a bad mood last night, Tom?"

"I got a fucking ticket on the way home."

"What? That sucks, Tom. A ticket for what?"

"Speeding," he answered.

"Shit. How much was it?"

"Seventy-five bucks."

"Why were you speeding?" Kate asked.

"I just wanted to get home," Tom said.

"Well, I guess I shouldn't be mad at that. At least you were trying to get home fast."

"Yeah," he said as he got two coffee mugs out of the cupboard.

Kate said, "So you raced home, and when you got here, you were pissed off at everything."

He looked at her and nodded.

"That doesn't make sense, Tom."

He just looked at her and then poured coffee into the mugs.

"Too bad, honey," Kate said. "You missed a great dinner last night. I'll pack up the leftovers, and you can take it to work for lunch. Do you want me to cook you some breakfast?"

Tom kissed Kate as he handed her a cup of coffee. "Yes, please. I'm starving."

Smiling, she got a frying pan out from under the stove. As she cracked an egg on the edge of the pan, she asked, "Tom, were you mad last night because of the baby thing?"

"No," he answered.

Kate continued, "Because maybe we can have another baby in a couple of years. Just not right now, okay?"

"That's fine," Tom replied. He watched Kate while she prepared the breakfast and noticed her long, comfy, chenille robe. Oversized, it was Kate's favorite. With her hair pulled back in a clip, she didn't look as rested as usual. Tom drifted back into the previous day's conversation with Athena and wondered if his wife was unhappy with her life.

"Kate, are you bored with the kids and everything?" Tom asked.

"Bored? Well, things get to be routine sometimes, but I wouldn't say that I'm bored. Why do you ask, Tom? Are you bored?"

"No," he said, "but I would hate to think that our lives have become boring."

"We're not bored, Tom. We're just married with kids," Kate said as she cracked a second egg. Buttering the toast, she looked at Tom adoringly and said, "I love my life exactly the way it is. There isn't anything I would change." She walked over to the refrigerator, got the orange juice out, and started talking about Natalie's field trip.

Nothing else was mentioned about having another baby.

Seventeen

That Thursday morning while getting dressed for work, Athena stopped at her phone, hesitated, then dialed her mother's number. She was actually relieved when she got her mother's answering machine, because that meant that she didn't have to confront the demons she had left back in Chicago. It had been over three years since she had spoken to her mother, and she did miss her terribly. She could not imagine the confrontation she would have to endure, although she had managed to avoid it so far. Her mother would just have to let go of any ill feelings she had for her daughter. Athena was, after all, her daughter.

Later that day, after Athena signed another client up for the company, she dialed her mother's phone number again. She reached her mother's voice on an answering machine once again.

The next morning, Athena dressed casually for work in faded jeans, a T-shirt, and flip-flops—all carefully selected. At lunchtime, she retreated home to bathe, shave her legs, and change into clothes that would render any man helpless. She had gone to the tanning salon the day before, so her body was bronzed and her shiny, toned legs were incredible. She put on a dark-green, raw-silk miniskirt, closed-toe stilettos, and the bra. The bra that could make any man forget who he was. The bra that, if worn by the right woman with the right blouse, could lure a man out of his recliner in the family room and into Athena's bed—naked.

Athena was, of course, that woman who bought the right blouse because she was after the wrong man. The man who was in love with his wife. The man who had a family, children he adored, and a life for which he worked hard. The man who would see her body staring at him, as if it were asking him to make love to it.

Athena knew the power of attraction. She knew what a man would give up for desire in that fleeting moment. She knew that when the right woman knew how to seduce a man, any man, he would fall. That woman might never enter his life, but if she did, she could pull him away from any other woman, any family, anytime.

Athena knew her accoutrements were over the top. The outfit, which pushed the envelope, could be pulled off only with the right attitude. She entered the office with her auburn hair in a ponytail, sporting black sunglasses and long, bare legs. She went straight to her desk as if on a mission, picked up the phone, and started dialing clients.

The sound of her voice caught the attention of Tom, who had been vigilant for her return. She waited for a moment when everyone appeared to be focused on their work, and then she maneuvered her way into Tom's office. He was at his desk, facedown in paperwork, when he heard the sound of an employee shutting the door behind her.

"Tom?" the familiar, sultry voice asked, "would it be okay if I left an hour early today?"

He lifted his head and asked, "Why? Do you have a date?" He had barely gotten the words out when he noticed her nipples reaching out to him. He fought the urge—but lost the battle—to stare her up and down. The faint smell of her fragrance was the ultimate aphrodisiac. She almost made his heart stop.

"Yeah," she said, "do you think it would be all right if I left a little early?"

Tom couldn't stop himself from complimenting her as he jokingly said, "You'll have her at hello."

"What? Oh." Athena giggled at his joke, and then paused. "Tom, there's something I have to tell you. Please don't get mad." She looked straight into his eyes and said, "I'm not a lesbian."

Tom looked at her as if he hadn't heard her.

"I'm straight as an arrow, Tom. I *love* men," Athena said. "My date is with a man I met a few weeks ago."

Tom almost lapsed into a coma, realizing that his safety net was gone. This woman, whom he found amazingly attractive, loved men. This woman was working in his office, and he couldn't get his fucking mind off her. "What about the strip joint?" he asked.

"Yeah," she said with a grin, "we had a blast, didn't we? You wouldn't have gone if you had known that I'm straight, and I really felt like you needed a night out." She jiggled her body slightly. "I'm sorry, but it's just that with every job I've ever had, there's been some guy lurking in the corner. I'm never interested, and I always end up unemployed. I'm sure it's happened to every girl here."

Tom sat there thinking how the women in his office wore three-inch-thick bras, and that he'd bet his life that it never, ever, happened to any of them.

"I'm doing really well here, don't you think?" Athena asked.

"Yeah," he answered.

"So I've got this hot date and I'm trying to look cute. I don't know which is tighter, my bra or my ponytail." She smiled at him.

Tom thought to himself, *She's wearing a bra?*

Then Athena asked, flaunting her fabulous thighs, "So do I?"

"Do you what?"

"Do I, like, look hot?"

Trying to cloak his answer, Tom responded, "Uh, yeah."

Batting her eyes, she asked, "So is it okay if I leave a little early?"

"Oh yeah, sure, of course. You've been doing great." He put his head back down and pretended to be immersed in his work.

Later, when she left, Tom noticed a lull in the office. He left shortly after her, and all the way home, the only thing he could think about was Athena and her nipples. The more he thought about her, the more the excited ache in his stomach became apparent. He felt himself getting turned on thinking about the way she moved. He imagined her unbuttoning her blouse and dropping it to the floor. He wondered what her breasts looked like and what it would be like to pin her against a wall and kiss her uncontrollably.

Tom was immensely aware of what he was feeling. It was as if he had suddenly awakened from a deep sleep and was excited to be alive. The only thing he wasn't feeling was guilt. The sexual attraction he was feeling toward Athena was too powerful and too intense to give any room for anything else.

That Friday night, Tom couldn't think about anything except fucking Athena. Kate tried audaciously to get his attention, but she couldn't get past his vague responses. When they finally got into bed, Tom reached over, pulled Kate underneath him, and kissed his wife profusely on the lips. He shoved his tongue into her mouth and kissed her hard, almost careless about what she was feeling. It was about Tom and Athena—Kate's body was just a vessel for his passion. He pressed his hands to the sides of her face as he made strong, thrusting motions toward her body. His suggestions turned her on, and they made passionate love, which ended quickly.

Afterward Kate lay there breathing rapidly from exhaustion. Smiling, she said, "Wow, that was amazing. You were quite the master there, honey."

Tom was breathing hard and staring at the ceiling. "What?" he asked, not sure what she had said. "Oh yeah," he said with a grin.

"Is everything all right, Tom? You always seem so preoccupied lately."

"Yeah, everything's fine. I'm just tired." Tom lay there with his eyes open, feeling sexually unsatisfied and frustrated. It was the first time in eleven years that he wanted to be lying next to anyone other than Kate. Still, the desire to be with another woman, something different and challenging, was exciting.

"I love making love with you, Tom," said Kate adoringly.

Tom responded, "I love making love with you, too."

Then he realized, *That's it! I don't want to make love—I want to fuck!* He wanted to fuck her brains out. He wanted to rip her clothes off in some hotel room and throw her on the bed, shoving his tongue down her throat while she rested her legs on his shoulders. Unfortunately, the woman in his fantasy wasn't Kate. It was the woman in his office, the woman who was not gay. She was the beautiful, exciting, funny, jiggling, fucking woman who was distracting him from his family.

Tom felt like he was under a spell. He looked over at Kate's content face resting on the pillow. He loved her so much and was feeling bad for the thoughts he was having. An overwhelming feeling of guilt consumed him for the rest of the evening.

Kate and the kids were his entire life, and nothing would ever come between them. *What am I thinking? What an idiot I am! She's hot, but so what? I love Kate. I will never, ever cheat on Kate. Not ever. I'm going to have to get this shit out of my mind or let Athena go. Nothing is ever going to happen between us.* Exhausted, Tom finally went to sleep.

It was early Monday morning and Tom had already been at the office an hour before the first employee showed up. Gradually the office filled with employees, and the voices of Athena and Thelma Rochen caught Tom's attention. He breathed a sigh of relief, which conflicted with the butterflies in his stomach and the excitement in his chest. Tom was lusting, and there was no getting around it.

That afternoon, most of the office staff were going to lunch together. Brian poked his head into Tom's office and said, "Hey, you going with us to the new Stuffed Potato?"

"No, I have a lot to do here," Tom answered.

"You want us to bring you back something?" Brian asked.

"No, I'm gonna get something at Whole Foods. Thanks, though." Tom picked up his phone and continued working on his computer. A few minutes later, the office was silent. He felt solace in having the place to himself.

Getting up from his desk, Tom stretched and yawned. Then he walked to the office lounge, where he found the only thing he wanted to see at that moment.

"Hi," she said, sipping bottled water.

"Hey," he replied as he walked toward the refrigerator, trying to appear unaffected. Tom's heart was pounding hard. He wanted nothing more than to kiss this girl hard.

Athena was attracted to Tom as well. She wanted the victory, but she had a physical need for him too.

A few moments of idle chatter passed before he asked, "So how was your big date?"

"Oh, it sucked." Athena saw a hint of relief on Tom's face, so she gave him a sultry grin in return.

He immediately turned his attention back to the refrigerator, pretending to look for something to eat. Athena rose from her chair and walked toward him. His heart started to race as she stood next to him. She bent down alongside Tom, forcing him to notice her bare thigh protruding from her shortened skirt.

They both stared into the refrigerator, a powerful tension between them. Athena reached in and pulled out a yogurt that she had placed there earlier. "These are delicious," she said slowly. "I get them at the health food store." Her flawless skin was perfect as she locked eyes with him.

Tom's breathing became more intense as he watched her tongue caress her lips. He looked down at her breasts and back into her eyes. His erection was noticeable as he became overcome with desire. His wife, kids, and everything in his life flashed through his mind as he fell helpless to the puissant feeling between his legs.

Tom felt as if a powerful drug had entered his body—his body that wanted Athena. His large, pulsating penis wanted her, and at that moment Tom wanted her. There was nothing that anyone could do to change the way he felt right then. This was the single, definitive moment in Tom and Kate's life, the moment that would change everything forever. Tom leaned toward Athena and placed his lips on hers. They began kissing with aggressive force and fell over onto the floor, giving in to the incredible lust they had for each other.

Athena gained control over Tom, rolling him onto his back and getting on top of him. She lifted her skirt to her waist and untied the two little strings on the sides of her panties that held them together, making them easy to remove. She pulled them off gently and placed them on Tom's face as she unbuttoned her blouse. She didn't remove her blouse, but unsnapped the front hook of her bra to expose her plentiful breasts. Tom was in ecstasy.

The next few moments of their insidious, powerful lovemaking were among the most exciting moments in Tom's life. His orgasm took him into a new world of sexual satisfaction. Something about the cheating and the forbidden fruit heightened the sexual gratification to epic proportions. He had never been so sexually stimulated, ever.

Afterward, Tom lay over Athena as they both enjoyed the physical contentment. He focused for a minute on a coffee mug that had been left on the counter by Brian, and then quickly got up and composed himself. Tom looked into Athena's eyes, kissed her gently, and then walked back into his office and closed the door.

Athena dressed quickly and tied her hair back in an elastic band. She grabbed her dark sunglasses from her purse and slipped out the door in victory, not returning for the rest of the day.

For the rest of the week, Athena was very low key, making herself scarce in the office. Tom did the same, skipping the office meeting that week and making sure not to make eye contact with Athena. But every night when he left the office, he thought of nothing else but that irrepressible, intimate connection he had with Athena. He couldn't escape that sexy image in his mind of her silky, voluminous hair falling in front of her face as she slipped down to cup his penis with her lips.

Tom was sitting on the den couch and staring into space when his thoughts were interrupted by a familiar voice calling out to him.

"Tom, dinner's ready," Kate said.

Without a word, Tom got up and walked to the table. Throughout dinner, the kids talked and giggled, but Tom didn't seem to hear a thing. He just sat there picking at this food.

"Tom," Kate asked, "are you okay?"

"Yeah," he answered without expression, glancing at Kate. "I'm not hungry, but I'm fine. I think I'm just gonna go upstairs."

Tom got up and went to their bedroom, where he lay on his bed and thought about things that had happened. He thought about what he was going to wear the next day and how he wanted to look. He felt excited about going to work the following morning.

Just as Tom started to drift off to sleep, he felt a nudging at his ear. He awoke to find Kate lying next to him in the dark, her hands caressing his head as she began kissing him. Tom wasn't feeling the desire at all. He would go through the motions, but only because of the guilty feeling he had over the woman who was consuming his world.

He kissed Kate back, and she grabbed his hand and placed it inside her panties. He slipped his fingers between her labia without enjoying the feeling of her moist flesh. Kate smiled as she waited for Tom's reaction to her newly shaven pussy, something she hadn't done since before Tyler was born. But Tom didn't say a word. He just kept going, oblivious to anything different.

Kate didn't say anything, but she found it weird that Tom didn't mention it, especially because it was so obvious. She wondered why her husband was so disinterested in her and their life lately. She loved Tom so much and she knew that he loved her too. She would just give him the space he needed to figure out what it was he was missing in his life, and then they would work on their family together.

The next morning, Tom took his time getting dressed. He wore his favorite dark-blue, long-sleeve shirt and shaved his face to start a goatee. When he got to the office parking lot, he checked his hair in the rearview mirror. He got out of his car and surveyed the lot for Athena's car. He was disappointed that it was nowhere in sight. *The situation must be getting to her,* he thought to himself. It was not like her to be late.

"Good morning, everyone," he said as he rushed by the receptionist desk and straight into his office. For the next thirty minutes, Tom tried to remain focused on his new accounts. But actually he was anticipating the arrival of the woman who was at the center of his distraction.

Finally, he couldn't stand his curiosity any longer. He walked out into the staff office, past Athena's vacant desk, and into the lounge. Phil and Barbara stood there sipping their coffee and talking about the day's upcoming events. Tom walked over to the cupboard to pull out a cup for himself.

"Anyone know why Athena's late?" he asked in an authoritative tone.

"No," said Phil, "but Brian does. He spoke with her earlier."

Tom looked out into the office at Brian, who was at his desk and apparently entrenched in a phone conversation with a client. Just then the front door to the office opened, and Tom looked immediately to see if it was Athena. But it was just Marge returning from the restroom.

Brian finished his phone call and had barely replaced the receiver when Tom said, "Brian, Athena called in?"

"Yeah, buddy," Brian said quietly, standing up. "I would have told you sooner, but I was on that call from New Haven for over an hour." He paused and then said, "I don't think she's coming back. I just don't know. She sounded hysterical."

"What?" Tom asked, concerned about what Athena may have told Brian.

"Well," Brian said, "I don't know, man. She's coming back, but I just don't know when. Her mom died, so she was headed back to Chicago."

Some of the other employees, who had overheard the conversation, made sympathetic noises. Tom just stared in disbelief.

"When she first called," Brian explained, "she said she would be gone indefinitely. But I persuaded her to take her time and come back when she's ready."

Tom was overcome with deep emotion—disappointment that he would not see Athena that day, and fear that he might never see her again.

He began running through a gamut of emotions, which lasted throughout the day. He had a melancholy demeanor and retreated into his office, where he spent the rest of the day sitting silently at his desk.

Eighteen

Athena sat in her seat, almost motionless, as the plane endured a tremendous amount of turbulence. Her red, tear-filled eyes made her look scared at first glance. But when asked by the flight attendant if she was all right, Athena just barely glanced up and nodded.

After showering earlier that morning, Athena had tried once again to contact her mother, only this time reaching an unfamiliar voice. Athena recalled asking if she had reached the right number. The woman who answered the phone told her that the lady who resided at that apartment had passed away several weeks ago. Athena just fell to her knees in sorrow. She couldn't believe that her mother had died without her even knowing.

Athena couldn't process the idea that her mother was dead. She was only fifty-eight years old. She wasn't sick, not that Athena was aware of, although she hadn't seen her mom in almost four years. How could so much time have gone by? Why hadn't she called her mother? She kept asking herself that question over and over again as she remembered the last time she saw her mother in the pew of St. Marcus at Joliet's wedding. She had tears of shame running down her cheeks.

Athena faced the rest of the flight with the horror of never being able to see her mother's smiling face again. That was surely worse than her plane crashing to the ground.

Throughout the flight, flickering thoughts of the erotic event that had happened between Athena and Tom passed through her mind. He was a much better lover than she had anticipated. A wicked smile crossed her lips as she remembered the look on his face when he noticed the piercing she had in a private location. She could always tell when a man had never seen anything like that before. Their arousal would always peak at that sight. However, the haunting thoughts of her mother's death disturbed Athena's exciting memory of that glorious afternoon in the lunchroom.

As the plane approached its destination, Athena thought of the chance encounters she might have during her stay in Chicago. The town was full of family and friends of David and Joliet. She was sure to run into someone who had been at the wedding. And what would she say if she came face-to-face with Joliet herself? Could she convince her friend that she had actually done her a favor? That the moment she met David, she had known that it would take only a casual hint of flirtation to get him into bed?

In reality, she had played her game long and hard to get David to stray from Joliet. And when it was over, he realized he had made a tremendous mistake. He felt the destruction of their love from the guilt he experienced almost immediately.

Triumphantly, Athena thought she had empowered the sultriness that ultimately provoked David to destroy his relationship with Joliet. She had thought it ridiculous for Joliet to give up so much of her life at such a young age, especially when she and Athena were having so much fun. However, Athena had never intended to tell Joliet that she had slept with David. She would have kept that secret to herself, smugly thinking of herself as the smarter of the two.

Maybe she could persuade Joliet to see it the way she did. Maybe Joliet could come to see that Athena had saved her from a lifetime of infidelities, and that Athena was not to blame for the wedge that came between David and Joliet.

Athena sat there feeling no responsibility for the consequences that may have resulted from her escapade with David. Those consequences were surely the result of his attraction and action toward another woman. The committed man could not be faithful forever when tempted by the right woman. Athena knew she was that woman, at least for most men.

After collecting her bag, Athena walked briskly through the airport wearing her faded baggy Levi's and an old Grateful Dead T-shirt. She carried her heavy leather overnight bag over her shoulder. Her white baseball cap and aviator sunglasses covered her sad, reddened eyes. Landing in Chicago brought back the harsh truth that she would never see her mother again.

She got a cab almost immediately, and during the ride through the familiar streets, she noticed all the changes that had taken place while she was gone. Riding down Glendale Avenue, she noticed that she was approaching the large church that had been so much a part of her life. The cabdriver had almost passed it when Athena called out, "Stop!" Startled, he looked back at her.

"I'm sorry," Athena said, "but could we stop here for just a moment? I just want to run in for a quick look."

"Sure, go ahead," the driver said in a Chicago accent.

Athena walked up to the church, looking at its rooftop as if seeing it all for the first time. As she entered the rear of the empty church, she remembered all the times she and Joliet had stood in line for Communion, seeing who could make each other laugh first. There were so many memories of the two of them—running around the church, hiding from Sister Maria, and ditching choir class. Still, the most deeply engraved memory was that of Joliet's wedding.

As she stood at the front of the church, she stared at the enormous crucifix that hung over the altar before her. She could smell the faint aroma of incense, usually used at funerals. Casually, she turned back to look at the pew where her mother had been standing the last time Athena saw her.

"She was your best friend, Athena," a husky, familiar voice said.

Athena turned quickly to see Father Callahan standing behind her. She swallowed as she stared at the once attractive, now older priest.

"He wasn't right for her," she said. "Obviously he wasn't right for her."

"I meant your mother, Athena," he said in a low voice. "She always did everything for you."

"I loved my mother," Athena said with conviction.

"I know," the priest said, "but she needed you, Athena. At the end, she was really sad."

She looked back at the priest, searching for some kind of logic in what she had done, but she couldn't find any. Without saying anything else, she walked down the aisle to leave the church.

"You should go by the apartment, Athena. There are boxes there, if they haven't cleared them out already."

Athena kept walking as if she hadn't heard him. When she got outside, she ran down the steps of the church and indicated to the cabdriver to leave quickly.

He sped off without an address, sensing that she was upset. After a few minutes, he asked, "Where do you want to go, miss?"

"Turn left up here on Palomino," she said quietly. When he turned left, she continued, "Make another left at the light. It's that brownstone on the right."

The cabdriver pulled up to an old, four-story brick building. The street was lined with cars and trees that bloomed with pink flowers in the spring. The buildings were a mix of old and new, including some that had been torn down and rebuilt. The older buildings were refurbished, but still had the old, quaint style of the thirties. The building that Athena and her mother had lived in was older and smaller, overshadowed by other buildings in the vicinity. Their building had always been clean and pretty, though, and it had always smelled of something baking in the oven.

Athena stared at the old building and noticed a vacancy sign hanging in a front window. Was the sign in reference to her mother's place? She glanced around to see if anyone she recognized was still there and wondered about how they might respond to her. Athena wondered if she had made a mistake in coming home, but her curiosity about her mother's death and when she was buried made it imperative that she stay.

Athena paid the cabdriver and got out. Walking slowly up the short steps, she remembered all the times she and her mother had sat on those steps, waiting for Joliet to come over and play.

She stood for a moment outside the old wooden door, then opened it and stepped inside. A lot of improvements had taken place while she was away. As she walked toward the elevator, the door behind the office desk opened.

Athena turned to see the same woman who had worked behind that desk all the years she and her mother had lived there. Mrs. Hallowell had given Athena and Joliet milk, cookies, and great advice almost every day after school. Mr. and Mrs. Hallowell had only one son, and when he moved to Pennsylvania, Mrs. Hallowell had taken after Athena and Joliet. She would babysit on occasion when Athena's mom worked or just needed an afternoon to herself.

"Oh, Athena," Mrs. Hallowell said as she walked toward Athena and wrapped her arms around her. "I miss your mother so much. You know how I felt about the two of you," she said quietly, looking directly into Athena's eyes.

Athena stood there sadly, her auburn hair flowing from the white baseball cap. She asked, "What happened?"

Mrs. Hallowell said, "About three weeks before she died, she was complaining of feeling dizzy and weak. I kept telling her to go to the doctor, and she said she would if it didn't go away. I should have just made her go."

"But what happened?" Athena repeated.

"That Monday morning," Mrs. Hallowell said, with tears welling up in her eyes, "she came down those stairs and collapsed. She went into a coma, never came out of it, and died three weeks later."

"But what killed her?"

"She had diabetes, and no one knew. Not even her."

"Diabetes? But diabetes doesn't run in our family."

Mrs. Hallowell answered with a sniffle, "It was a rare case. Her low blood sugar, which she neglected all those years, turned into sugar diabetes."

Athena walked over to the window and stared out, as she had done so many times before. Then she asked sadly, "Are her things still upstairs?"

"Yes, I packed up most everything." Then Mrs. Hallowell walked over to the desk, pulled out a set of keys, and handed them to Athena. "Here, you go ahead. Take some time up there, and I'll come up in a little while."

Athena took the keys and without another word walked slowly upstairs. When she got to the top of the stairs, she turned down a long hallway and stopped at door 243. She stared at the number a moment, then put the key into the doorknob and unlocked it. She opened the door completely to expose the packed room and stood there quietly. The once comfortable, homey apartment now harbored labeled boxes and tainted happy memories of long ago.

Athena walked in apprehensively and gently put her hand on the arm of the flowered sofa. She remembered the happy day when she and her mother picked it out. They had both loved it and agreed it was the prettiest sofa either of them had ever seen.

She walked around the apartment and into the bedroom that had once been hers. Among the many boxes on the floor, she noticed one that was sealed and marked with different tape and writing. In her mother's handwriting, it was labeled "Athena pictures." Athena looked around for something sharp with which to open the box. In the kitchen she found a pair of scissors, right by the roll of tape. She walked back into the bedroom and opened the box.

She pulled out pictures of a very young Athena taken in grade school, and a photo album dedicated to the friendship of Athena and Joliet. One picture had the eleven-year-old girls in smiles and braids, making bunny ears over each other's heads.

From the bottom of the box, Athena pulled out a folded dress. Inside the dress was a framed picture and an old, stuffed, rag doll. The picture was of a three-year-old Athena holding that rag doll as she was hugged to the chest of her father. Next to him was her very young mother. The picture had been taken in the same moments as the framed picture in Athena's apartment. The picture in her apartment, of the happy Athena and her mother, had been taken by her father. Of all her mother's things that came into Athena's life, these would remain her most treasured possessions.

The memories of her past were interrupted by a knock at the door, which was partially open. "Hello," Mrs. Hallowell said.

"I'm in here, Mrs. Hallowell," Athena answered.

Mrs. Hallowell walked into the apartment. They discussed what they would do with the boxes and which ones Athena would take back with her. The conversation was brief, and nothing was mentioned about Joliet or David. Mrs. Hallowell did not see it as an appropriate time to bring that up, and Athena did not want to dig into that conversation.

Athena collected her overnight bag, indicating to Mrs. Hallowell that she was finished. Mrs. Hallowell looked confused and asked Athena where she was going. "I'm going to stay at the Hotel Bowman," Athena said.

"But Athena, please stay here," Mrs. Hallowell pleaded, taking Athena's bag from her. "We haven't seen you in so long. It will be the last time you'll be able to stay in that room, and you can take your time as you go through your mother's things." It took a few minutes, but Mrs. Hallowell won the argument. She left shortly afterward and closed the door behind her.

The following day, Athena went through boxes and tears, keeping the things she wanted and crying over things she had to give away. In the late afternoon, she came across her mother's address book and opened it up to Joliet's address, which was crossed out. Underneath it was Joliet's new address and phone number.

Athena contemplated calling Joliet, but instead she called a cab company and asked where the address was located. They informed her that it was about twenty minutes outside of Chicago, so Athena requested a pickup and got dressed.

Five minutes before the cab was to arrive, Athena called Joliet's number to make sure she was home.

"Hello?" a woman said.

Athena said nothing.

"Hello?" the woman asked again.

Athena recognized Joliet's voice, although it didn't sound as happy as she remembered. She listened to one more "Hello" before she hung up the phone. Then she checked herself in the mirror and went outside to collect her cab.

When Athena arrived at the address, she wasn't the least bit surprised at the extravagant neighborhood, which was typical of the Terranova lifestyle. Athena did not pay the cabdriver. Instead, she told him to wait until she had confirmation that she was welcome to stay.

She walked up the long brick walkway, pausing before ringing the doorbell to announce her arrival. The strong, loud chimes sounded almost pious, like the church chimes with which they had grown up.

An older lady, wearing a uniform dress covered with an apron, answered the heavy, ornate door. "Hello," she said.

"Hello," Athena replied. "Could I speak to Joliet, please? I'm a friend of hers."

The lady looked out at the cab and then back at Athena, concluded that she was not a threat, and told her to come inside and wait in the foyer.

As Athena stood there for a moment, she could overhear Joliet asking the woman who was waiting for her in the foyer. But before the woman could turn back to get the information, Athena was standing behind her.

Joliet froze in despair, face-to-face with the woman who had changed her life forever. Athena was equally shaken, looking into the bloated, once-beautiful face of Joliet.

Finally Joliet responded to the shocking—but not unexpected—return of Athena. "I knew you'd be back," she said softly, "because of your mother. But I didn't think you'd come here."

Athena stood there, trying to grasp the change in Joliet's appearance. Then she slowly said, "You would have never been happy with him."

Uncontrollable rage came over Joliet and she screamed, "How do you know? How can you possibly know what would make me happy? You took everything from me, and then you left," she said sadly. Then she looked up at Athena and her eyes welled up in tears. "I loved you so much. I loved you!" she yelled.

"I love you too," Athena said.

"No!" Joliet yelled at her. "Don't tell me that you love me. You don't know anything about love."

"Yes, I do. I didn't want to see you get hurt." Athena couldn't help but notice that Joliet's once youthful appearance was gone.

Intensely angry, Joliet yelled, "Didn't want to see me get hurt? You fucking bitch, you're out of your mind." She walked over to the window and continued, "I have been nothing *but* hurt for the past four years. And you come here, without compunction or a touch of conscience, expecting me to forgive you, like we're gonna be best friends again? You pathetic bitch."

Looking Athena up and down, Joliet noticed that she still looked beautiful despite the tragic loss of her mother. "Obviously you haven't been affected by the past four years like the rest of us have."

Athena took a deep breath and said, "Yes, I have."

"Oh really? Has anyone told you where David is?"

"No. Why? Did he leave Chicago?"

"Yeah, he left Chicago. He's in prison for vehicular manslaughter." Athena gasped as Joliet continued, "After the wedding, or supposed-to-be wedding," she added hatefully, "he tried desperately to get me back, but I couldn't go back with him. It could never be the same. David developed a drinking problem. He was out with his girlfriend one night, after I got married—"

Athena interrupted her. "You got married? To whom?"

"Nobody you know. It lasted only a year and a half. He liked to hit me." Joliet looked away before continuing, with obvious sadness, "Anyway, David got in an accident and his girlfriend was killed. It was his third offense, so he's in prison for a long time."

Athena felt a sinking feeling in her stomach.

"Everyone's doing great," Joliet said facetiously. "David's in jail, I'm on antidepressants, and your mother died." She really wanted to hurt Athena.

Athena yelled, "I had nothing to do with my mother's death."

"Woohoo, a tragedy you had nothing to do with. You may not have caused her death, but you weren't there when she died!" Joliet walked up to Athena and looked her straight in the eyes. "Tell me something, Athena. At our prom, when Clayton disappeared for twenty minutes, we joked about him screwing someone in the bathroom. It was you that he fucked, wasn't it?"

"No, that's ridiculous!" Athena shouted.

"Oh really? Then why were you gone at the same time? Back then it never crossed my mind that you would do something like that, but now I know you. Just get the fuck out of my house!"

As Athena grabbed her purse and started walking toward the door, Joliet yelled, "You're just like your father, Athena. Just like him!"

Athena ran to the cab and told the driver to leave quickly. Returning to her mother's apartment, she spent the rest of the evening on the coach in the dark, vowing never to return to Chicago.

Nineteen

It was Monday morning and more than a week since Athena had been in the office. For Tom, it had felt more like a month. As he drove into the parking lot, he looked for Athena's car, as he always did. He felt a hint of excitement when he thought for a brief moment that he saw it, but he was mistaken.

As he walked past Athena's desk, Tom glanced at it briefly to see if anything had been disturbed, which would indicate to him that she might have come back. Then he went immediately to his desk, picked up his phone, and checked his messages. He passed over all of them quickly when he realized that none were from Athena.

For the next few days, Tom thumbed through papers that were piling up on his desk. When he went to lunch with Brian, he hardly spoke or ate. He tried to shrug it all off, blaming his lethargy on not feeling well and being overworked, but he knew that the real reason was that Athena was gone and he missed her.

At home, he was even more distracted. He argued with Kate over his belligerent attitude toward the kids, and she told him how disinterested he seemed in everything the past several months. He tried hard to pay attention to everything around him, but all he could think about was Athena and that powerful afternoon in the lunchroom.

Once again, he went up to bed early that evening and pretended to be asleep when Kate retired. She had noticed the distance between them and how long it had been since they had made love. She lay in bed worried about her husband, and thought how nice it would be if they could get away for some time alone together. She finally fell asleep trying to figure a way they could do just that.

The next morning when the family was at the table enjoying breakfast, Tyler accidentally spilled Tom's coffee as he reached for the milk. Tom went unusually ballistic. Tom and Kate were volatile with each other, and the children ran upstairs crying. Gathering his briefcase and wallet, Tom sped off to work. Frustrated, Kate was left to clean up the mess. Once again, he had left without a kiss.

Tom faced another chaotic environment at work. Two employees were jumping on him for answers, and Mrs. Roth was transferring a call from an irate client to his desk. As he walked into his office and picked up the receiver, he was ready for another argument. He finished the call in anger and immediately noticed the red light on his phone flashing, indicating a new voice message. Entering the password, he heard the sound of the voice for which he'd been waiting. An instant sensation of excitement filled his chest.

"I miss the lunchroom," she said in a quiet sultry voice. "I didn't think I would speak to you again after what happened. But I'm so sad right now, and I thought the sound of your voice would make me feel better. I hope you're okay." Then she hung up.

Tom replayed the message three times just to hear her voice. Suddenly the ponderous grief was lifted and he was happy again. He focused on every word she spoke, listening to it each time as if hearing it for the first time.

When he hung up, Tom stared straight ahead. Smelling his fingers, he recapped every moment in the lunchroom with a smile. He felt aroused and alive, trying to remember the scent of her pussy. The fact that she had called him, and that he was so excited to hear her voice, was invigorating to him. She turned Tom on in a hard way, and he couldn't wait to have sex with her again.

Twenty

It was midweek and Kate was at the grocery store, shopping for ingredients for the fabulous meal she was planning to prepare that evening. It had been a long time since the family had had a great dinner together, and she thought it would be nice to cook lasagna, Tom's favorite meal.

As she walked down the personal-hygiene aisle, she pondered the idea of buying a home pregnancy test. It seemed kind of silly, she thought, but it had been more than a month since her last period, and she had been feeling nauseated. She hesitated and then put the test back on the shelf.

That evening when Tom got home, Kate had a beautiful Italian dinner waiting for him on an authentic red-and-white-checked tablecloth. The family ate and laughed together and the children shared stories about their day. It was a cozy, intimate evening that had been desperately needed in the Verdi home.

After dinner, the family sat on their fluffy couch, eating hot fudge sundaes and giggling over home videos. Tom laughed and was content being with his family, but still he couldn't stop thinking about Athena.

The next morning, Tom grabbed a cup of coffee from the lunchroom before going to his office. When he turned on his computer to check his e-mail, he was ecstatic to see one from Athena: "Hi, Tom. I'll be back to work tomorrow. I have been working on my laptop and have two serious deals coming in on Friday. I'll make up for my missed time, I promise. Athena."

Tom loved the seriousness of her e-mail. The fact that she was concentrating on work and could put two deals together in her situation was impressive to him—and she hadn't mentioned the lunchroom. It was going to be an interesting and tantalizing week.

The next morning Tom was in the office exceptionally early, dressed nice and wearing his favorite cologne. Promptly on time, Athena walked in wearing a cream-colored pantsuit and high heels, with her auburn mane pulled back in a ponytail. She walked to her desk and caught Tom's eye immediately as she stood there for a brief moment. Their eyes locked, until someone grabbed Athena's attention with their condolences.

Afterward, Athena walked into Tom's office and closed the door. He was enchanted with her presence.

"Hi," she said softly.

"Hi," he replied.

She looked behind her to make sure no one was watching. "I'm sorry about what happened. Can we forget it and move on? I really love my job here." She stood at the door and smiled a sexy red grin.

The magnitude of Tom's attraction for Athena was distorting his self-control. He knew at that moment that he should fire her, but he didn't. Instead, he answered, "Yeah, it never happened." But he knew deep in his brain that it had. There was no way in hell that he could ever forget that day in the lunchroom.

At that very moment, he was remembering her tiny panties on his face and wondering if she was wearing the same kind right then and there. Nevertheless he pretended it was all in the past and that they would move on.

The rest of the week was exciting to Tom. He kept his head down in his work, but sneaked an occasional peek at Athena. At home, she was all he could think about. There was nothing again mentioned about the lunchroom, and when Athena's deals came in, they celebrated with a distant hug.

On Sunday afternoon, Tom and Kate were walking through the mall with their children. They had just finished lunch when Tyler and Natalie noticed a toy store and ran inside. Tom and Kate followed them. They stayed in the toy store for quite a while, and when Kate noticed Tom becoming impatient, she motioned to the kids to hurry up. They chose their toys and all walked out happily.

A few stores down, Tom noticed a lingerie store. The mannequin in the window was wearing panties similar to what Athena had worn on that memorable afternoon. "Hey, babe," he said to Kate, "let's go inside here." Tom walked into the store without waiting for her to answer. He went over to the panties hanging on the T-rack and pulled off the pair in front without checking the size. "Get these," he said to Kate.

She looked at them without saying a word, and then checked the price tag. "They're thirty-two bucks," she said as she started to put them back.

He took them from her. "So what? Just get them."

Kate looked at him in amazement. "Thirty-two dollars, Tom? You always tell me never to spend money on lingerie because you prefer me naked," she said with a sexy grin, waiting for Tom to validate what she had said.

Natalie and Tyler giggled. Kate had forgotten for a moment that they were right there. She made a cute little gesture to them as Tom took the underwear to the counter.

"Wait," Kate called out. She pulled out her right size and exchanged them for the ones Tom was holding. He paid the cashier and then handed the bag to Kate with a smile. She thanked him, and the family walked out together, all holding hands.

Later that day, after Tom barbecued on the grill, he helped Kate clear up the dinner mess. She was standing in the kitchen when he walked up to her and whispered in her ear, "Go upstairs and put on those panties that I bought for you."

She smiled seductively and said, "I already have them on, Tom."

Excited, Tom immediately reached underneath her sundress. "Go upstairs," he whispered as he slid his tongue in her ear. Kate dried her hands and quickly went upstairs.

Tom put a kids' movie in the DVD player and then sneaked upstairs. When he got to their bedroom, Kate was on the bed wearing only the panties. Tom undressed, lay down on the bed next to Kate, and then pulled her on top of him. They kissed briefly and then Kate started to slip the panties off.

"No," he said firmly, "untie them."

Kate smiled. "These don't untie, honey."

"Yes, they do. Untie them," Tom insisted.

"They don't untie," Kate said again.

Then Tom reached down to untie them himself. He fumbled with the string and after a few moments realized they were not going to untie. They resembled the panties that Athena had worn, but they were not exactly the same. Frustrated, Tom ripped them apart and the two began kissing passionately.

In a breathy tone, Tom asked Kate to remove her panties. When she did, she held them out to her side and then, after a moment, dropped them.

At another time, Tom would have thought that to be insanely erotic. But after his encounter with Athena, nothing else could compare. Unknowingly, Kate was in competition with another woman for her husband's erotic obsessions. She never knew that while her beautiful Tom was making love to her, all he could think about was fucking another woman.

Kate's world was no longer her own. Her husband's heart belonged to her, but his brain, blood, and penis belonged to Athena, a woman Kate had never met—at least not to her knowledge. She was losing her husband to someone who had seen a picture of a happily married couple and decided to slither in between them. Athena was destroying Kate and Tom's lives by devouring the rock-solid bond that had held them together as one. Kate never even knew what was happening.

Several days later, Tom was at the desk of Lucy Cavali, an older woman who had started with the company earlier that month. Lucy was doing very well, and Tom had taken her under his wing in an effort to stay busy and keep his mind off Athena. When he returned to his office, his phone was flashing the red light, indicating that someone in his office wanted to speak to him. Tom picked up the receiver and was elated by what he heard.

"Come to my house tonight at eight thirty," she said in a sultry, breathy voice. "I want you in my mouth, Tom, just one more time."

Tom wasn't prepared for her invitation or his reaction to hearing it on the phone. His body was aching to kiss her as much as it was to be inside her. He fantasized about kissing her, over and over again in his head. He hadn't felt that kind of yearning to kiss Kate in a long time. He loved Kate, but the kissing had become perfunctory, as it does in every relationship.

It was as if Athena was pleading with him to fuck her, and the fact that she wanted it as much as he did turned him on even more. He could feel the blood rush to his hardening penis at the thought of another encounter with her.

Before he could say a word, she asked, "You know where I live, don't you? I'm at the Stevo Villas, 29720-D."

"I can't," Tom said.

"I need to be with you," Athena insisted.

"I can't, Athena. I'm married."

She said more sternly, "Why can't you? We've already had sex. There isn't anything we can do that we haven't already done. Just come over. I want you."

Her persistency made Tom feel an insanely strong desire to cave in, but he knew he couldn't. In his mind, there was absolutely no possible way he could go to Athena's house. As much as he wanted to go, he would have to put it out of his mind.

Still she persisted. "I'll make it so worth your while, Tom."

"Athena, this isn't gonna work," he said, hating himself for the words coming out of his mouth.

"What isn't gonna work?" she asked? "You coming to my house and having the best sex of your life?"

"No, you and me working together. That's not gonna work."

"Well, I'll tell you what, Tom. I'm going to leave, and if you can pass up a night like tonight, then maybe you're not the guy I thought you were."

Curiosity made him ask, "And what kind of guy is that?"

"The kind of guy who, on his eighty-year-old deathbed, isn't wishing that he hadn't pass up the fuck of the century."

"I'll take my chances, Athena." Tom stared at her through the glass window, as she whispered into the phone and tried to convince him of the spectacular sex they would be enjoying.

To her disappointment, Tom turned her down. But before she hung up the phone, Athena made one last attempt. "I'm at 29720-D. My door will be unlocked."

"I'm sorry, Athena, but I won't be there. You'll have to find another job." Tom felt sick, as if all the joy had been sucked out of his life. He couldn't believe he had actually told her to find a new job. He knew it was the right thing to do, but still he didn't want to make her leave. What else could he do? Have an ongoing affair and cheat on his wife? He loved Kate too much, and he had always loved making love to her until this passionate obsession came into his life.

How had this happened? Tom pondered the events of the past several months. How did he get so dissatisfied with his life and so interested in another woman? He had never cheated on any of his girlfriends. Before this happened, he would have bet his life that he'd never cheat on his wife. Even before he met Kate, he would have bet that. He had always thought that when he got married, that would be it—he would never cheat. He had had the willpower before Athena. Tom had had sex with many women in his past, but when he had committed to a relationship, he had never cheated. It just wasn't in his character. He valued his relationships much more than that—and he respected women, his marriage, and his wife.

In the past, he would always break up with a girlfriend if it got to that point. He would never disrespect someone like that. His parents hadn't raised him that way. They had been married almost fifty years and no one came between them, at least not as far as he knew. Tom felt ashamed of himself when he realized how deeply into this mess he truly was. He decided to finish up his work and get an early start home.

When Tom arrived home, Natalie was asleep on the sofa and Kate was in the kitchen talking on the phone. He walked in and gave her a kiss on the cheek. She was ordering patio furniture for the backyard when Tom caught the price.

"Thirty-eight hundred dollars?" he said, alarmed. "We really don't need that right now."

Still on the phone, Kate looked surprised. She whispered, "I thought you said you wanted it. What the hell, Tom?"

"I know, but it just seems expensive right now."

"But it's summer and we don't have anywhere to sit out there." Frustrated, Kate said to the salesperson, "You know, I'm gonna have to call you back." Then she hung up.

They bickered for a while, until Tyler came running in the kitchen all excited to see his dad. He tried to talk to Tom about his exciting day at water camp, but Tom just looked through him, not as interested as he would have been in the past. Kate cooked dinner, and the two went back and forth about the patio furniture.

As she sliced the tomato for the salad, Kate reminded Tom about her outing with the girls that evening. "Remember, I told you? At seven, I'm taking the kids to Karen's and they're sleeping at her house. The moms are going to that chick flick, *Skinny Man in a Blond Suit.*

All Tom could think about was the red-haired naked woman waiting for him, and he knew this wasn't a night to be on his own. "Kate, I was hoping we could be together tonight. Stay home, can't you?"

She kissed him on the cheek and said, "Believe me, hon, I'd love to. I don't feel like going out tonight."

"Then don't."

"I have to, Tom. It's my turn to drive, but I'll be home early." Then Kate smiled and added, "Don't worry, I'm not spending the night."

Dinner was quiet. Kate reminded the children to mind their manners at Karen's house, and she went over the details of the evening. "Make sure you tell Kyle's daddy thank you for everything, and make sure you always share your toys with Kyle." Natalie and Tyler were excited about their sleepover.

Tom just sat there with a burning ache in his stomach. He couldn't help thinking about what could be in store for him later that night, if he chose to go.

Upstairs, Tom stood at the door to Tyler's bedroom. He watched Kate take out the tiny Spider-man pajamas and put them on the matching bed as Tyler jumped out of the tub. "Mommy!" Tyler yelled with a big grin as he ran to her waiting arms holding a fresh warm towel. Kate always warmed the towels before the kids got out of their bath. She dried Tyler off and kissed his nose. Mother and son smiled at each other as Tom watched.

Tom was wrestling the demon inside him and trying to decide what was more important to him. He had an uncontrollable desire for another woman, and her invitation to him for that very night was too enticing for him to easily turn down. But he knew that he would have to turn her down and continue to suffer from his weakness for her in silence.

Shortly after, he walked into his own bedroom and caught Kate slipping on a pair of comfortable cotton panties and pulling a long billowy skirt over them. She put on a tight short-sleeve sweater, and she looked lovely. He walked up to her from behind and kissed her neck.

"I'll be back a little after one o'clock, honey," Kate said, kissing Tom on the lips and grabbing her purse. "C'mon guys, let's go," she shouted to the children.

As Kate and the kids hurried out of the house, Tom tried to ignore the butterflies he felt escalating rapidly in his chest. "Have fun," he said as Kate helped the kids out the door and into her Range Rover.

"I'll see you later, honey. Bye!" Kate said. She had no way of knowing that she would never see *that* Tom again. After that night, things would be different.

Tom watched his family pull out of the driveway, and then a sudden wave of excitement hit his body with a jolt. For the first time in his life, he was unsure of himself and what he was capable of doing. He was shocked at his choices, but this unfamiliar version of himself was invigorating to him as well. He felt attractive and sexy in a way he hadn't felt in years. He was refreshed and revived, and he wanted to do something dangerous. On his last day on earth, Tom didn't want to regret missing out on this.

Tom wanted the death-defying roller-coaster ride, the bungee jump, the incomparable thrill that only the most exciting night of raw sex could bring. He didn't consider the fact that the reason those things are so exciting is that they all involve serious risk—paralysis, death. Or even worse, Kate could find out, in which case he would lose his family forever. But all Tom could think about was the barbaric curse of the Kama Sutra.

Tom took a longer-than-normal shower and shaved his face extremely closely. He put on his favorite aftershave, the one Kate always said turned her on without warning. He combed his dark hair to the front, a change from how he usually combed it, because he remembered Athena mentioning something about a man looking sexy with his hair combed forward.

He walked over to his closet and pulled out the white, long-sleeve, button-down shirt that he always got compliments on, and he paired it with his faded blue jeans. He pulled his black leather slip-on loafers over his clean bare feet. Afterward he clipped his fingernails neatly, and then went under his wife's sink to retrieve her nail file for a smoother finish. He looked at himself in the mirror and approved of what he saw. He hadn't put that much effort into his appearance in a long time, and his self-confidence was at an all-time high.

What Tom was feeling had nothing to do with Kate. It was nothing she had done or not done. It was all about life and the way that marriage evolves over time. The comfort level that married people strive to achieve is the very thing that will drive a wedge between them. The excitement that had driven Tom and Kate together had gradually dissipated, thanks to babies, diapers, and happy times at the mall.

Good morning kisses and good night hugs erode the passionate experience that we feel with a stranger. The stranger becomes the lover, the lover becomes the wife, the wife becomes the friend, and no matter what, the inevitable happens. The hot, steamy, dirty sex becomes familiar, and that familiarity kills the excitement of the unknown. It's the not knowing what comes next, the spontaneity, that is at the very heart of passion.

Tom, in a small way, was a victim. He was the man who met the wrong woman. If Athena hadn't entered his life, he would have remained faithful to his wife through their entire marriage. He would have remained dedicated to his family and never even considered the idea of cheating on Kate. But Athena had the ability to turn him into someone he didn't recognize. Her mere existence rendered him helpless. Nevertheless, he was about to make a crucial decision that would affect the lives of everyone he knew.

Tom walked downstairs and grabbed his keys off the counter. He turned off all the lights and walked out to his car. He started it, but before driving off, he put in his favorite Pink Floyd CD, *Dark Side of the Moon*, and played "The Big Gig in the Sky." When he was a kid, that was the song he would listen to when nobody was home. He would turn it up loud and imagine he was with the most voluptuous woman in the world as he pleasured himself. In his fantasy, the woman always had auburn hair, much like that of his third-grade teacher, Miss Rothers.

Tom drove out of the neighborhood to a local restaurant and bar. He walked directly over to the bartender and ordered a shot of tequila and then another. He tipped the bartender and walked out. He drove down the road until he approached the Stevo Villa town houses. He pulled in and found a vacant parking spot. He looked at his clock and saw that it was 8:23.

He sat there a few minutes and noticed how beautiful the night was. The light from the sunset outlined the California mountains that surrounded the town of Thousand Oaks. The temperature was just perfect, and everything felt serene. It was the ideal setting for a date with a stranger, and Tom wanted to be part of it. His conscience was weighing on him, but he was engulfed in the magnetism of Athena and powerless over his attraction for her.

He slowly opened the door, got out of his car, and locked it with his key. He walked a short distance before seeing the number 29720-D. As he approached Athena's town house, he got an overwhelming feeling of nervousness. He stood at the door for a moment and took a deep breath. He was going to knock, but then he stopped. Instead he opted to open the door and enter without permission.

Entering the town house, Tom quietly closed the door behind him. He glanced around the opulent setting, which was obviously decorated for his arrival. Dozens of lit candles were everywhere—big ones, little ones. There were even candles on the wall. A beautiful smell of food cooking captured his attention, although there was no cook in sight.

The subtle sound of belly-dancing music came from an open door. As Tom walked slowly across the living room toward that door, the anticipation was titillating. He could see the flickering light of a burning candle inside. Tom had a sense that he would be welcomed, but he hesitated since he had entered Athena's home without permission. Still, he felt a surprising level of comfort with her—and after all, it was eight thirty, the time at which she had invited him.

The music was as sexy as the setting. Tom knew there was no turning back. Approaching the half-closed door, he eased it open with his hand. What he saw then stopped his breath in an instant.

Burning candles adorned the dark room. In the center of the fluffy, ample-sized bed was Athena, completely naked, her long red hair loose like a lion's mane. Her left arm was above her head and her legs were apart enough to show him her world.

She was completely shaven, which drove him crazy. He slowly walked closer to her to get a better look at her gold-jeweled piercing, which was in a place he didn't know women wore jewelry. The fact that she was so brazen with her body aroused him more than he had ever thought possible.

Noticing Tom's arousal at her piercing, Athena spread her legs even farther and touched herself with her fingers. He glanced down at the piercing and then back up at Athena. Then he put his hands on her knees, gently spread them apart, and whispered, "We're gonna fuck our brains out tonight."

He kissed the inside of her knees, down the inside of her thighs, until he had his tongue wrapped around the little piercing. As he began kissing it, Athena groaned loudly. They didn't stop until the moment Tom had to leave, and when he left, he did so only because he had to.

Tom had a restless night. He tossed and turned and woke up several times, staring into the dark night for hours. He was sleeping next to Kate, but all he could think about was what had happened in Athena's bed.

The next morning, he was exhausted. Kate woke him up, but he could hardly remember where he was at first. As he showered, Tom realized that he was in too deep—too deep to forget about Athena, but too deep to see her again.

He had feelings for her, with every fiber in his body. He was obsessed with the thought of her shiny hair flowing over her face as she sat nude on top of him, her hands pressed tight against his chest as she smiled her sexy grin.

Athena was so different from Kate. Kate was wonderful in bed, but Kate was his wife. With Kate, it was making beautiful love together. With Athena, it was insatiable fucking. Athena was the forbidden fruit, and forbidden fruit is always sweeter.

Driving to work, Tom wondered how it was going to be when they saw each other again. He was as nervous as a schoolboy, and he didn't want to fire her. She was the only thing in his life that was giving him excitement at that moment, and he wasn't willing to give it up just yet. Pulling into the parking lot, he didn't see Athena's car. But he briskly headed into the office to get a head start on his day.

At home, Kate cleared away the coffee cups and got the kids interested in a video. Then she went upstairs into her bathroom and got out the home pregnancy test she had purchased earlier that week. She went into the toilet and gave a sample. She was nervous and excited, and she felt good about what she was doing. The phone rang, and she set the test on the counter as she ran to answer it. It was Karen.

"Hey, what's going on?" Kate asked. They talked about the movie, and after a while Kate confided in Karen how tired Tom had been lately. They giggled about marriage, and then Kate ended the call. She was eager to read her result, and when she walked back into her bathroom, she saw it immediately. Kate couldn't have been more thrilled. Her test result was positive. Kate was pregnant.

Twenty One

Kate got dressed as fast as she could. She was so excited about the pregnancy, and she hadn't realized how happy she'd be to have another child so soon. This was just what her family needed, and she knew how happy it would make Tom.

She got the kids fed and dressed, and then hurried out to the car, which was parked in the driveway. When she put her key in the ignition, it wouldn't start. She tried several times, but the car had a dead battery. Becky, her next-door neighbor, walked over when she noticed Kate was having trouble getting her car started.

"What's going on, Kate?" Becky asked.

"I don't know," Kate answered, obviously upset. She tried again and then got out of her car. "I don't believe this. It was fine last night. I just really wanted to go see Tom."

"Is everything okay?" Becky asked.

"Oh yeah, everything's great," Kate said with a smile. She pulled Becky aside and whispered, "I wanted Tom to be the first to know. I'm pregnant."

Becky replied with a huge burst of excitement, "Ohhhh, that's wonderful. Take my car, Kate. Go ahead, and just leave the kids here with me," she insisted.

"Are you sure, Becky? I really don't mind taking them."

Becky walked back toward her house as Kate followed. "Leave them here with me," Becky said, "and you two go for a romantic lunch. Then tell him."

"That's a great idea, Becky," Kate said. "Thank you so much," she said, to her gracious neighbor. She took Becky's car keys and waved goodbye with gratitude.

Tom was in his office when the flashing light on his phone appeared, indicating that someone was waiting to speak to him. He picked up the phone and heard her exciting voice.

"Tom, it's me. I'm out in the parking lot."

"Why are you in the parking lot?" he asked.

"I want to talk to you alone. We need to talk," she paused, and added, "Come outside."

Tom said, "Okay."

Kate was sitting in the parking lot of Tom's office building, ecstatic about her secret. As she grabbed her purse from the passenger seat, her cell phone rang. It was Becky asking if she could take the kids to the pool.

Kate was on her cell phone in a car that was unfamiliar to Tom. Meanwhile, Athena was out in the parking lot, waiting for Tom to come out and talk to her. During Kate's phone conversation with Becky, the attractive woman standing outside her car caught Kate's attention. Athena was dressed in cut-off shorts and a braless tank top, but she inarguably looked fantastic.

"Holy shit," Kate said out loud.

"What?" Becky asked.

"Oh nothing," Kate said. "There's just this hottie woman standing outside Tom's office—one of those women, you hope your husband never sees."

Becky asked, "Oh, you mean Miss Big Tits Tiny Ass?" They both giggled.

A few seconds later, while Kate was still on the phone, she saw Tom walking out of his building toward the woman leaning on her car. Athena stared right at him with a flirtatious look on her face. Watching Tom walk toward Athena, Kate sensed that something was wrong. It was obvious that they were familiar with each other.

Kate quickly ended her phone call with Becky. As she watched Tom walking toward the woman, Kate noticed something different about him. He had a gleam in his eye and a smile that she had thought belonged only to her. He looked at the woman without blinking an eye, and in an instant Kate knew that her family was in jeopardy. She could hardly breathe as she sat silently, watching her world being turned upside down.

Tom and Athena greeted each other, and the sexual tension between them was evident, especially to Kate. They were standing in each other's space and it was indisputable—they were more than just casual acquaintances.

Kate sat there with her mouth open and her heart in her stomach. Tom's leers at Athena's body, and his obvious concern to make sure no one was watching, validated what Kate was surmising. All the pieces were coming together as Kate observed Tom and Athena's interaction with each other, when they thought no one else was watching. Tom picked a tiny flower from a bush nearby and handed it to Athena.

Kate could hardly believe what she was witnessing. Finally, she blurted it out softly. "Oh my God, she's sleeping with my husband." Suddenly everything made sense—Tom's disinterest, his drifting, his disconnection, the lingerie store, everything exposed. Kate was devastated.

"I can't believe this is happening to us," she told herself, feeling hopeless. She was pregnant and her husband was having an affair. "I can't fucking believe this," Kate said, staring at her husband as he moved a strand of hair out of Athena's face. Athena was giggling, and it was all Kate was finding it nearly impossible, not to jump out of her car and scratch Athena's eye's out. But she was determined to remain calm. She had to compose herself; otherwise she would act irrationally and not handle the situation the way that she would ultimately want it handled. So she sat there crushed, with tears pouring down her heartbroken face silent in her agony.

Tom's conversation with Athena was casual and flirtatious. He never dreamed that the love of his life, Kate, was a witness to it. His involvement in the situation was plain for anyone to see, and Kate was destroyed.

She sat in her car until Tom and Athena finished their conversation. Then Tom walked quickly back into his office, and Athena drove off— followed by Kate. Athena stopped at a drugstore and then at a market for a few groceries. Kate stayed close, like an experienced private detective.

When Athena reached her Stevo Villa town house, Kate pulled in behind her. She watched as Athena parked her car and walked into what looked like her villa. Kate couldn't see the number, but she made note of exactly where it was.

Then Kate went home, gathered her kids from Becky's house, and cried for hours. Tom had gone back to his office and daydreamed about Athena, never knowing the measure of pain he had caused. On the surface, everything appeared to be normal at the Verdi home.

The following Saturday morning, Kate got up early after a bad night's sleep and checked Tom's cell phone for messages. There had been nothing out of the norm all day. Through the night, she continued to keep a close watch on his phone messages, but nothing came up until the following afternoon.

Tom was in the shower after being in the pool with the kids. Kate checked his cell phone and noticed there were two new messages, one from the office and the other from Athena.

"Hey, it's the goddess," Athena's message said. "Come by my house at three o'clock this afternoon." After a short giggle, she continued, "I'll make sure it's worth your while."

The goddess? Kate thought, *What the hell is that?* She couldn't believe what she was hearing. Even though she had seen what she had seen in Tom's office parking lot, she had still hoped there was some misunderstanding. But now the truth was confirmed—Tom was having an affair. He was cheating on Kate, and she was aware of it. Kate deleted the message.

It was 1:45 p.m. and Kate had remained upstairs wondering who this woman was and how Tom had met her. She wondered how long the affair had been going on and whether Tom loved the woman. Kate had a thousand questions, none of which she wanted answered. After all, she had seen the young woman, who was blatantly sexy and an obvious threat to any marriage.

After a while, Kate took a shower and got dressed. She told Tom that she needed to run an errand but that she would be back shortly. She wondered what she would do or say, but she wasn't sure. She felt desperate and curious. She wanted to confront the vixen who had entered their home, and she was not going to be calm and rational about it any longer.

Kate got in her Range Rover and drove down her street, feeling lonely. Pulling down her sun visor, she caught a glimpse of the picture she and Tom had had taken together at his Christmas party. She pulled the picture down, crinkled it in her hand, and tossed it to the backseat. Picking up speed, she then drove directly to the Stevo Villas.

Kate parked in almost the same spot in which her husband had parked a few nights earlier. She remembered the door that the woman had walked through, and she sat staring at it for a moment before she finally stepped out of her vehicle.

She wondered if Tom had been there, and she began to imagine what must have happened inside the villa if he had. She felt rage, remorse, and embarrassment all at the same time. She was sad for her children and for the baby she was carrying inside, and she began to feel sorry for herself.

Kate got out of her black SUV and started walking toward the town house. As she approached the front porch, she looked around with curiosity. She put her fist out to knock on the door and then noticed the peephole. She stopped, because she didn't want to take the chance that the woman would avoid the confrontation.

Suddenly remembering the invitation on her husband's cell phone, she angrily tried to open the door. It was unlocked, and she pushed it open with ease. Reluctantly, she walked in slowly, totally unprepared for what she was about to see.

To her stupefaction, she found the woman lying on her stomach on her sofa, wearing only thigh-high nylons, stilettos, and a baseball cap. Her elbows supporting her upper weight, she swung her high heels back and forth, obviously waiting for a man—Kate's man, Tom Verdi. Kate couldn't help understanding Tom's attraction to this stunning sexpot. She couldn't believe that this woman was waiting for *her husband*.

Athena was equally stunned as she rose quickly and covered her breasts with a pillow. She and Kate had met briefly in Santa Barbara. Kate didn't remember Athena, but Athena remembered Kate from the picture she had stolen from the office.

"Well," Kate said in a sarcastic tone, "wrong Verdi, huh?"

The two stared at each other for a moment. Athena was slightly embarrassed and didn't say a word.

Kate asked, "Who are you? And how did you meet my husband?"

"I work with Tom," Athena said.

Stunned, Kate said, "You work with Tom? Are you new?"

There was a silent moment, and then Athena answered with a vengeful smile, "I'm Athena, Kate."

Kate was confused and began to wonder if she had made a mistake about her husband. "You're Athena?" she asked, desperate for an explanation of what she had seen in the parking lot. "But you're gay, aren't you?"

Athena asked, "Did your husband tell you I'm gay?" In a flaunting gesture, she pulled the pillow aside as if to show Kate what Tom had been enjoying. "Your husband would know, better than anyone, that I'm not gay." She lay back down on her side and said smugly, "Ask him."

Kate threw open the door and ran outside. She drove around her neighborhood for more than an hour, crying and trying to figure out what to do. She didn't know who to turn to or where to go, so after a while she just drove home.

When she walked in the house, she could see across the room into the backyard. Tom was out there playing with the kids. He was distracted with them, so Kate ran upstairs and threw cold water on her face.

Staring in the mirror, she couldn't believe how her life had changed in a matter of hours. It felt surreal, as if she were living a nightmare.

Kate wondered if Athena had called Tom to give him a heads-up.

Either way, she was going to confront Tom that night, and she cried over the thought that it could lead to the demise of her family.

Kate lay on her bed with her tear-stained cheeks and puffy eyes, staring into space until she briefly dozed off. She had gotten very little sleep the night before, and she was exhausted from the grief she had suffered. Only a few moments into her slumber, she felt a nudge on her arm.

"Mommy, are you sleeping? Come downstairs."

Kate opened her eyes and saw Natalie standing next to her bed, holding her doll. Kate pulled her daughter closer so she could give her a hug. "I love you so much, Nat," she whispered. Then she asked, "Does Daddy know I'm home?"

"I don't know, Mommy. Do you want me to go tell him?"

Kate said, "No, I'll be down in a minute, honey." She got up and walked into the bathroom, where she splashed more water on her face. Then she walked over to the phone to call her parents.

"Hi, Dad. I'm good." Kate kept the conversation with her dad brief, and then she asked to speak to her mother. "Mom," she whispered, "I need a huge favor. Could you come over and get the kids? I need you to take them for the night." She emphasized the urgency of picking up the children as soon as possible, and she asked her mother not to ask any questions. Kate would explain later. Without hesitation, her mother was on her way.

Kate stayed upstairs as long as she could, until Tom realized she was home.

"Kate!" he yelled upstairs. When she didn't answer, he yelled again, "Kate!"

Kate yelled back down, "I'll be there in a minute, Tom." She had been in the kids' room getting an overnight bag ready for them. She was no sooner done than she heard her mother's car pull up outside. She yelled out the window, "Mom, I'll bring the kids out to you." Her mother, confused, didn't ask any questions.

Kate called to her children, who immediately came running to her in the living room.

Tom followed behind, and he looked stunned when he noticed the overnight bag in Kate's hand. As Kate was kissing the kids, Tom asked, "Are the kids going to your folks' house?"

"Yes," she said, opening the front door.

Tom could see his mother-in-law standing outside her car, and he asked why she didn't come inside.

Kate ignored Tom's question and walked the kids out. As Tyler ran to his grandmother, she scooted him and Natalie into the car. Kate just looked at her mother, gave her a hug, and said she'd call her in the morning.

Kate's mother was concerned, but she knew that she shouldn't press for answers. So she just drove off without saying a word.

When Kate got back in the house, Tom was standing at the kitchen counter cutting up lemons. He smiled at Kate and asked, "Are you planning a romantic night for us, hon?"

"No," she said, "I thought I'd leave that to you and Athena."

Tom stopped dead in his tracks. His mouth dropped open, and the look on his face said it all. He couldn't believe that Kate knew.

They stared at each other for a moment, and then Kate said, "The other day, I thought I'd go have lunch with my husband. Instead, I found him in love with another woman."

"I'm not in love with her," Tom said.

"Oh, so you just love fucking her." She stared right into his eyes.

Tom didn't answer. He wanted to lie, but he didn't. He just stood there, validating his wife's suspicions.

"You sorry son of a bitch," she said. "You had everything. You had everything *here*! What more could you possibly have wanted?" Kate's face was wracked with pain.

"Kate," Tom said as tears began to well up in his eyes, "I love you so much. I don't know what happened."

Furious, Kate screamed, "You don't know what happened? I'll tell you what happened—you put your dick in someone else. That's what happened! You got caught. That's what happened!" Then she started to cry and could barely get out the words, "I thought you were happy with me, Tom."

Tom was crying too. "I am happy with you, Kate. I love you. I'm sorry."

Full of anger, Kate yelled, "You can't just say that you're sorry. You lied to me the whole time. You told me that she was gay."

Tom said, "I thought she *was* gay. She told me she was."

Kate was enraged. "Now that dirtbag has ruined our lives."

"Don't call her a dirtbag," Tom said. "She's not like that."

Kate was devastated. "You're going to defend that slut?" She began to walk frantically through the living room and back into the den and kitchen. "I can't believe this. You're throwing our lives away for that scumbag."

"I'm not throwing our lives away," Tom cried out.

Kate screamed back, "I saw her, Tom. I went to her apartment."

"What?" he asked.

Kate could barely get the words out. "She left you a message on your cell phone—an invitation for another fuck. When I got there, she was waiting for you, Tom," she paused, "and all she had on was a baseball cap."

Tom stood silently.

Kate cleared her throat and said, "That afternoon in the lingerie store … and then later, you trying to untie the panties?"

Tom was embarrassed. It was all unveiled.

"I could never look at you the same way, Tom." Kate began to sob. "You were my everything." She ran out of the room and up the stairs.

Tom was devastated. He had never dreamed that this would ever come out, especially not today. He saw the devastation of his actions, and he had never felt so bad in all his life. Everything was destroyed, and he was to blame for all of it.

He wondered if anyone from his office knew. If Kate found out, maybe someone in his office knew as well. He thought about how much he loved Kate and his children, but still he couldn't stop thinking about Athena. He knew he would have to give her up. As much as he didn't want to, he knew it was over.

That night, Kate didn't sleep in their bed. She tried to sleep in Natalie's bed and then in the guest room. After tossing and turning all night, she went downstairs and sat in the dark living room. She stayed there alone for hours, sobbing and reminiscing about old times.

Then she heard Tom coming downstairs. He was wearing only his pajama bottoms, and his eyes were puffy from crying. He stood there with his arms hanging to his sides, feeling vulnerable and helpless. How could he have done this to the woman he loved? Everyone he knew would be affected by it, especially his precious children.

"Kate," he said gently, "I can't believe I've done this. I just want to die."

"I want you to die too," Kate said, "and take that bitch with you."

He tried to apologize to her, but she was unreceptive. Before long, their voices had elevated to loud yelling. Kate was standing by the fireplace and crying hysterically while Tom tried to tell her how much he loved her. Kate asked Tom if he loved Athena. He said no, but he wasn't convincing and Kate was disgusted with him.

Tom tried to make Kate see it from his point of view, but that only infuriated her more. He looked around the room for anything that would remind Kate how great they were together and what a beautiful life they had.

"I wasn't the one," Kate said, "who forgot how great our life was, Tom, remember?"

In a desperate attempt, he pointed to the snow globe on the fireplace mantel. He tried to get Kate to remember how exciting it was when they were first dating. She stared at the beautiful snow globe for a moment and then, in a fit of rage, picked it up and raised it above her head.

Tom screamed, "No!" but it was too late. The glass was shattered, water was everywhere, and the magical snow had disappeared. The broken pieces signified Tom and Kate's life now—and their broken hearts. Once again Kate ran upstairs crying and feeling hopeless, leaving Tom and the broken snow globe behind.

The next morning when Kate got up, she found the snow globe on the kitchen table. Tom had spent half the night gluing the tiny pieces back together. He had managed to put it together except for the glass, water, and snow. Little Tom and Kate were still in the truck, and their hot chocolates were still intact.

Kate remembered that night and how she had felt. She remembered Tom and how much in love they had been. It had seemed like nothing could ever come between them. She had felt as if she had captured the rainbow, as if no one in the world had what she and Tom had. What had happened between then and now? What *had* come between them?

Meanwhile Tom was out in the garage getting his rake out for the gardener. Becky, his next-door neighbor, could see him from her yard, so she walked over and said, "Tom, I'm so happy for you guys.

Tom wasn't going to answer. He didn't know what she meant, and he didn't care.

"Anytime you need me to babysit, just let me know," Becky said.

Tom still didn't know was she was talking about. He started to walk away, but then Becky said under her breath, "It'll be nice having another little baby in the house." Tom took a couple of steps and then stopped. He turned back to look at Becky, dropped the rake, and ran into the house.

He ran through the living room and into the kitchen. When he didn't see Kate, he ran out back and then upstairs to their bedroom. Then he ran down the hall and found her in the laundry room. She was holding Tyler's T-shirt to her face and sobbing. Tom grabbed her and held her closer and longer than he ever had before. They cried together until they could cry no more.

Tom didn't say a word. He kept his arms around Kate, and they walked together into their bedroom and lay down together. He held her close for hours, until the pain they were both feeling subsided a bit. When Tom put both his hands on Kate's stomach and looked into her eyes, she realized that he knew she was pregnant.

It had been several months since Kate had fold out Tom was sleeping with Athena. During that time, she had told him several times that she wanted to raise the baby on her own. She constantly struggled with the pain caused by the wedge that had developed in their marriage, but she knew in her heart that she still wanted Tom in her life.

As Kate was driving around their neighborhood, in the distance she could see Tom out in the street in front of their house. He was playing catch with their son, Tyler. Natalie, their daughter, was on the sidelines wearing the little cheerleader skirt that Kate had made for her the previous Halloween. Tom and the kids looked happy, and for a moment, it looked like nothing bad had ever happened.

Kate kept her foot on the brakes for a moment, watching them, and for the first time in a long time she felt content. Tom had been teaching Tyler how to catch a football, and the two of them had been bonding lately. Natalie was playing cheerleader, and they were all laughing and having a good time.

Tom hadn't thought about Athena in weeks, and things seemed to be mending between him and Kate. But Kate still felt the pain every so often, the kind of pain that your heart feels when it knows it has been betrayed. The kind of pain that tells you that you're not that special, you're not that loved. The kind of pain that feels like it will never go away completely. Kate felt that pain every time she was reminded of her strong love for Tom, knowing that things could never be the same.

She would think about the times he had been with Athena, daydreaming about what must have taken place. It was difficult for her to get those images out of her head. The hardest part for Kate was knowing that when her husband was with Athena, Kate was the very last person on earth he wanted to see. Anyone in the world could have walked into that room, and they wouldn't have been more unwelcome than Kate. It killed her to know that.

As Kate sat there watching her family, she tried to savor the moment. *My family*, she thought. *Mine!* She didn't want to give it up, but at that moment, she didn't know if she and Tom could stay together after what had happened. She truly didn't know if she had it in her to forget or forgive, but she would try.

Kate drove her car forward slowly, watching her family and knowing that she and Tom had a long road ahead of them. She would try to make her marriage work, but it was going to be on *her* terms. Everything would be different now; everything was going to be her way. She was no longer the same Kate. She was stronger, harder, and different. *Everything* was different.

As she slowly drove up the street, Tom and the kids noticed her car. They all greeted her with the kind of hugs that every wife and mother wants. And they walked into the home together—Tom and Tyler first, then Natalie and Kate following behind. She closed the door and they all walked into the kitchen for a drink, all except for Kate.

She stood in her living room, the one she had taken so much love in decorating, and walked to the fireplace. She looked at the broken snow globe, the one she had once loved so dearly. It was placed on the center of the mantel, and it really seemed to reflect their life now.

Still, Tom and Kate were together in their little truck in front of the beautiful crystal-covered lake, holding their yummy hot chocolates. And a drip that would be wiped away, by that pristine mitten. And all the magical elements that made a perfect evening, for two people to fall in love.

Kate smiled as she remembered how the twinkling snow used to fall, like a blanket covering them in their chilly times. How she loved that snow globe.

But the magical snow was gone now, and like their lives, no matter how they tried to put the snow globe back together, it would never be the same. The shelter was gone, and the music didn't play. It would always be a broken snow globe, with the beautiful memory, of how the magical snow used to fall.

THE END

Printed in the United States
By Bookmasters